THE
ASCENDING

Tor books by T. M. Wright

THE
ASCENDING

T. M. Wright

TOR

A TOM DOHERTY ASSOCIATES BOOK
NEW YORK

THE ASCENDING

This book is printed on acid-free paper.

A Tor® Book
Published by Tom Doherty Associates, Inc.
175 Fifth Avenue
New York, N.Y. 10010

Tor ® is a registered trademark of Tom Doherty Associates, Inc.

Library of Congress Cataloging-in-Publication Data

Wright, T. M.
    The ascending / T.M. Wright.
       p.   cm.
    "A Tom Doherty Associates book."
    ISBN 0-312-85729-2
    I. Title.
    PS3573.R444A9   1994
    813'.54—dc20   94-606
                                     CIP

First edition: August 1994

Printed in the United States of America

0 9 8 7 6 5 4 3 2 1

For Becky, who, like Ryerson, is out on a limb.

And for Sheba, a barrel of love.

THE
ASCENDING

RYERSON BIERGARTEN

When he was fifteen years old and had discovered his psychic abilities, Ryerson Biergarten was positive he'd gone crazy. He knew about people who "heard voices," or saw faces in the wallpaper, or woke night after night from the same awful dream. So when that sort of thing started happening to him, he went to his mother and said, "Mom, if you're a minor and you're crazy, do they put you away with the grown-up crazies?"

She looked at him silently for a moment. She was very perceptive, and he was positive that she knew at that moment just what was afflicting him. She said, "Are you afraid, Ryerson?"

The question surprised him. He said, "Yes," paused, and added, "How'd you know?"

"I can see it in you," she answered. She was at the sink, peeling potatoes. The water was running while they talked, and later Ryerson's memory of their conversation would be colored by the sound of the water running—as if, again in his memory, they were talking at the edge of a waterfall. She was wearing a blue flower-print, knee-length dress, and her very long blond hair was tied with a red ribbon to keep it out of the potatoes.

Ryerson said, "I see things, Mom." He shook his head in confusion. "I see things and they come true." He paused. "Or I find out later that they're true."

"And you think you're crazy because of it?" she asked.

It was a rhetorical question, but he answered, "I don't know."

She nodded. "Tell me what you see, Ryerson."

Ryerson shoved his hands into his pockets. He was in many ways a typical sixties teenager, growing up in the suburbs just outside Boston. He was something of a slob, a trait he never grew out of completely. He was fascinated by the Beatles, Herman's Hermits, and the Rolling Stones. His schoolwork suffered from his preoccupation with girls, basketball, and acne. So, when his mother looked around at him with a quizzical expression on her face and said, "Tell me what you see, Ryerson," what *she* saw was an awkward, vaguely-scared-looking young man whose brown corduroy pants were baggy, whose shirttails hung out, and who was beginning to sport what might generously have been called a mustache. At the same time, this archetypal teen-age boy was suffering torments that few other teenagers suffered, and she knew it.

Ryerson said to her, "I see all kinds of things, Mom," and added hastily—because he knew that she despised vagueness—"I saw that Charlie was going to get hit."

Charlie was their dog. He had been hit by a school bus a week earlier and was recuperating in the garage. He had a broken leg and what would later be revealed to be a cracked pelvis.

"When?" Ryerson's mother asked and shut the water off.

"The day before it happened."

She turned around from the sink, folded her arms over her chest, sighed, and sat at the kitchen table. "And what else?" she asked.

"And what else?" He was confused. "Don't you want to hear about Charlie?"

"We both know about Charlie."

He looked at her for a long moment until it became clear what she was saying: they both knew about Charlie, so he could be lying. Ryerson clasped his hands nervously on top of the table. He didn't like being mistrusted by his mother. He said, staring at his hands and pouting a little, "And I know that Dad and you are going to get a divorce."

Her expression froze.

After half a minute, Ryerson said, "Mom?" He read pain in her. He felt her pain and her heartache. "Gee, God, I'm sorry," he said.

His mother stood, stared appraisingly down at him, nodded, and said, "Never let anyone tell you that what you have is a 'gift,' son. It isn't."

RUNNERS

In the summer of his sixteenth year, Ryerson saw a camel on a dirt road near his uncle's farm.

It was his first runner. He didn't have a name for it then. He didn't call it a "runner." In those few seconds after it appeared, he saw it simply, if bafflingly, as a camel. It was facing him from ten feet away, and it was chewing happily with that slight, odd smile that camels seem to have. Its big, heavy-lidded eyes were half-closed, and it moved its front legs forward and back slowly, as if impatient. As its hooves hit the dry dirt, they sent up small clouds of dust. When the dust settled, there were hoofprints in the road.

Ryerson hadn't expected to see a camel in the Massachusetts countryside. He had been looking for a copy of C.S. Lewis's *Out of the Silent Planet* that he'd lost somewhere between his uncle's home and Levitt, the closest town. He'd walked to Levitt because his uncle had wanted a six-pack of Rolling Rock beer and had explained wearily, "The day is too awful damned hot to go out driving." So Ryerson had volunteered to walk into Levitt—two miles away—to get the beer. He took the book to read while he walked. He finished it halfway there (he had already read it a number of times) and put it in his pocket. When he got back to his uncle's house with the beer, he found that the book was gone.

So, when the camel appeared, Ryerson was looking for his lost book and wondering why his "abilities," as his mother called them, were not helping him much.

The sudden appearance of the camel made him jump. The first thing he thought was that camels spit at people, and he didn't want this one spitting at him. He backed away from it a few feet, put his hands up at chest level, palms out, and pleaded with the camel to stay right where it was. He thought, of course, that it had gotten loose from some traveling circus. What else would a camel be doing on the road to Levitt, Massachusetts?

It blinked at him. He blinked back, though as a sort of reflex action, not as a way of trying to communicate with it. Ryerson thought that camels were very stubborn and independent and stupid. He was not going to try to communicate with such a creature. *It might get the wrong idea and charge at me,* he thought.

He said to the camel, "What the hell are you *doing* here?"

It blinked again, then shuffled impatiently. A fat honeybee buzzed over from the open fields nearby, circled the camel, then sped off into the fields on the opposite side of the road.

This is what Ryerson thought when the honeybee had lost itself among the thousands of honeybees in the fields of clover—he thought that it had buzzed right through that camel's nose.

As soon as Ryerson thought this, the camel shook its great, bullet-shaped head furiously, snuffled and snorted, and reared up on its hind legs like a horse.

Its underside was very much like a horse, in fact, and Ryerson thought that a camel shouldn't look like a horse underneath. He had never before seen the underside of a camel. He had seen the underside of a horse, though—his uncle had two horses that were very old and spent most of their time in a big fenced pasture behind the farmhouse.

The camel settled down, blinked again, shuffled about. Clearly it was waiting for Ryerson to tell it to do something, but Ryerson still had no intention of trying to communicate with it.

Before the camel's appearance, Ryerson had been walking in the center of the road with his head down. The road was very narrow, barely wide enough for one car, and he could get a good view of the shallow ditch to either side of the center. It was in the midst of a head-swing from left to right that he became aware of the camel—or at least that there was something very large in front of him.

That narrow dirt road was quite clean. Lots of people walked it. Ryerson had walked it several dozen times, but it was unusual to see any kind of litter on it—a beer can or discarded gum wrapper. The people who walked the road were country people, and littering was not their habit. So when Ryerson saw the empty pack of cigarettes in the ditch, he had stopped for a moment and stared at it. *Fine Turkish Tobaccos,* it read. And the word CAMEL arched over the side view of a camel. That was a good five minutes before his encounter with the impatient, snuffling beast on the road.

It was not until much later in the afternoon that he remembered the empty pack of cigarettes in the shallow ditch. Not until hours after the camel had turned and trotted off down the road and he'd followed it at a fast run, watched it lumber into the fields a good fifty feet, stop, and turn its great head to look at him, that odd smile increasing ever so slightly.

It had found his treasured copy of *Out of the Silent Planet.*

He told Uncle George about the camel. They were sitting at the kitchen table, playing rummy.

Uncle George was tall, stocky, and very strong. He liked to put on an appearance of gruffness, but his eyes were the eyes of a man who cared a lot about people. He cared so much about people, in fact, that he had become something of a recluse at the farmhouse.

Ryerson said to him, "I saw a camel on the road today."

Uncle George was in the midst of adjusting his cards. He looked briefly at Ryerson over the top of the cards and said, "Is this a joke you're going to tell me, Ryerson?" He put a card down, picked one up from the pile in the center of the table, and put it into his hand.

Ryerson answered, "No. I really did see a camel. It helped me find my book."

"What book?"

Ryerson told him.

Uncle George nodded. "That's a good book." He laid his cards facedown on the table and leaned forward. "You know," he said, "we got opossum, raccoons, deer, and foxes, and maybe even some wildcats around here, but we don't have any camels." He nodded sagely, picked up his hand, discarded one of the cards, and settled back in his chair.

That's when Ryerson remembered the empty Camel

cigarette pack in the ditch to the side of the road, because
Uncle George smoked Camels. Ryerson said, "I saw an
empty pack of Camels in the ditch, and a couple of
minutes later, I saw the camel on the road."

Uncle George smiled. "That's quite a damned coincidence, wouldn't you say?"

"It wasn't a coincidence, Uncle George. It happened."

Uncle George nodded. "And the camel turned round
and ran, and you went running after him, and the camel
found your book?"

Ryerson nodded. "Yes," he said.

When he was in his early twenties, Ryerson wrote to
himself: "The curse of this 'gift' is that *I* have it. Because
who am I? I'm not blessed with the wisdom or brilliance
that would allow me to use it properly. More often than
not, it is a burden, and it sits heavily on me.

"Even the dreams I have are . . . schizophrenic—like
watching a TV that's tuned to 85 different channels at
once. There is sense, and there is nonsense, but no
delineation of the two. They are dreams that have the
smell of decay and the touch of contentment, and the
hard whisper of panic in them—like sleeping in the gar-
bage of the rich.

"This gift threatens to turn me into an agoraphobic.
When I go out into the city"—he was living in a one-
room apartment in Durham, North Carolina, while he
worked for his doctorate in psychology at Duke University—"I am *blitzed* by the thoughts of those around me,
and it is all I can do to keep from wandering out into the

street and being run over by a truck because of it. Some of this psychic material is fascinating, much of it is pornographic—for lack of a better word—but the majority of it is damned disgusting. I got today, for instance, and very loudly, as if the person thinking it was in a panic— *My teeth, my teeth, I didn't brush my teeth!*

"Lately, however, I've been learning to shut out much of that sort of thing. At least I've been learning to sort what's important from what isn't, and when I've done that, my mind seems to take over and push the extraneous stuff aside. It's an ability for which I'm thankful, though I don't know the mechanics of it.

"One benefit of this gift is that I probably know better than most people, through firsthand experience, just how complex the mind really is, how many . . . rooms it has, how many of those rooms are open, how many are closed, and how many of those will probably stay closed forever.

"Not that I can assign a number to it. I can't say, *The mind has 1,000 rooms and five or six of those are open, the rest are closed, and 90 percent of those will remain closed forever.* I can't say that, but the numerical relationships are probably right.

"And the thing is, in all of those closed rooms there are influences that can seep out under the door, like odors, and find their way into the great open room of the mind, and influence *it.* Shape it. And so, shape us. I think it's something in one of those closed rooms that has made me able, at last, to sort out the useful from the junk and then push the junk aside. Something in another room has given me the gift itself that makes that ability necessary.

"Someday I think I'll be able to peer into the particular room where my gift originates.

"A fantasy comes to me. I see that there's a magician or a sorcerer in that room, and he sits in there and makes this gift work because it is, in reality, *his* gift and he's only sharing it with me out of perversity. This . . . entity is very amused by the whole thing.

"And then there's the problem of romance."

Ryerson stopped writing. It was painful to write about his love life.

He looked very preppy. Tweed sports coats and bulky sweaters, corduroy pants, and loafers were the clothes he found comfortable.

He had a square face, deep-set hazel eyes, a cupid's-bow mouth, and strong chin. He usually wore a short, badly trimmed beard, though he sometimes shaved it off for a month or two—once because a woman whose attention he desired thought, in so many words, *How can you trust a man with a beard?* He was told often that his eyes were his most interesting and expressive feature. He liked hearing that, though he wondered what feature other than the eyes were a person's most interesting and expressive. He was a shade over six feet tall and he carried himself with purpose and agility, though his posture was a little too erect, the result of overcompensating for a tendency to slouch.

Before going to Toronto to help the police in a search for a missing thirteen-year-old boy, Ryerson had been doing a lot of thinking about what many referred to as a "group mind." He found the concept fascinating. His version of the "group mind" tied in with his idea that the mind was composed of many rooms, that some of these rooms were open, but that most would remain closed and locked forever.

He had seen what he referred to as "the fog" more than once. This was a vaguely luminescent and amorphous entity which, he supposed, connected all living things, just as telephone lines connected houses. At first he thought that this fog gave people like himself their particular psychic gifts, that he, unlike most people, was able to tap into it and pick from it the information he needed. He discarded the idea quickly. He didn't "pick information" out of anything. Information came to him in a flood—only recently had he been able to sort the junk from what was useful, and even that was an ability he had not consciously developed.

It came to him that the fog did not so much *connect* minds as it was, itself, a kind of mind, or intelligence, and that the biological entities known as brains tapped into *it*. He believed, as well, that his gift was not actually the result of some talent he possessed, but pretty much the opposite: that his brain did not have the ability that most other brains did—the ability to discard the psychic junk that came their way so they could concentrate only on what the five temporal senses fed them. Otherwise, with that barrage of psychic information, the brain would have a hell of a time keeping even the *physical* world straight. Ryerson knew this only too well. It had taken a long time for his brain to automatically ignore much of the telepathic information coming his way so he could even cross a street without consciously sorting the relevant information from the irrelevant, the physical from the nonphysical. It was a task that most other brains, unfettered by a barrage of telepathic information, handled with ease.

Ryerson Biergarten had never smoked, and if he drank more than one or two glasses of scotch and water, or two or three beers, he got sick. He had gambled several times while in college, but there was no great attraction in it for him, so he hadn't done it since. His first wife, Eileen, told him once, "You know what you are, Rye? You're too *good.* Why don't you acquire some vices, for God's sake?"

Ryerson had shrugged, a little stunned by the proposal, and explained, "None of the usual vices appeals to me much, Eileen. Otherwise, I would."

She'd laughed at him. It had been what she considered a typical Ryerson Biergarten comment: slyly self-confident and self-effacing at the same time. "You are not as innocent and virginal and *good* as you believe you are," she told him.

He had nodded and grinned. "Yes," he said. "I realize that."

He wrote once: "As poorly as I know myself, as poorly as I know the complexities of the human organism, the mind and the brain, I know even less well what goes on unseen in the atmosphere around us—the stuff that gets into us and shapes us and makes us move. But, and I have to write this nonetheless, it is clear that *we're* a part of *it* and *it* is a part of us. It goes beyond symbiosis—just as the brain itself and the spinal cord do not have a symbiotic relationship, or the thighbone and the knee-cap. They exist *because* the other exists. They're all a part of the same damned thing!"

ONE

J ack Whitehead said to the cop on South Wacker Drive, "She went in there two hours ago"—he nodded at the 110-story Sears Tower across the street—"and she hasn't come out. Her name's Augusta Mullen." He began to spell it.

The cop held up his hand. "I can't do nothin' for ya, Mr. Whitehead. Sorry."

"What are you talking about? She's missing, for God's sake!"

"Two hours don't add up to missing. Hell, she could be in the can for two hours." The cop nodded at the Sears Tower. "Why don't you go in there and find her?"

"The doors are locked," Whitehead answered. It was 9:30 in the evening. The vast, smoky gray bulk of the Sears Tower rose into blackness.

"Right," the cop said and thought a moment. "Then this is what you do." He nodded at a phone booth, half a block away. "You go on over to that phone booth, and you call up whoever your girlfriend went in there to see."

"She's not my girlfriend," Whitehead protested. "She's my fiancée."

The cop handed Whitehead a quarter. "Okay, then, you go over to that phone booth and call up whoever your *fiancée* went in there to see."

Whitehead gave back the quarter. "I have my own money." He went over to the phone booth, looked up the number of Augusta Mullen's former husband, Wayne Volker—who had law offices on the 95th floor of the Sears Tower—and dialed the number.

"Wayne Volker here."

"Wayne, this is Jack. Is Augusta still there?"

"Is she *still* here? She never got here."

"She never got there?"

"That's what I said."

"But Wayne, I saw her go into your building more than two hours ago."

Wayne said nothing.

Whitehead coaxed, "Did you hear what I said, Wayne?"

"We have a point of logic here," Wayne said. "If Augusta really did come into this building two hours ago, she would have gotten here by now. So, *ipso facto,* she did not come into the building. She went somewhere else. She dumped you."

"That's not funny, Wayne. This is serious business. I saw Augusta go into your building." Whitehead felt someone tapping on his shoulder. He looked. The cop was standing behind him.

"So?" the cop asked.

"One second," Whitehead answered.

The cop nodded.

"Wayne?" Whitehead said. "You still there? Wayne? I've got a cop here with me. Do you think you could buzz us in?"

"Buzz you in? Jack, this isn't some east-side apartment house." He sighed. "Okay. I'll come and open the doors for you. Give me five minutes to get down there."

Frenzy was the word that fit. Like being on a merry-go-round that was out of control. Like being in a blender. Like being in a cement mixer.

A cement mixer?

"Hey, my man, whatchoo been doin', anyway?"

"Nothing. I'm a butcher."

"Yeah, and *I'm* the prince of fucking Wales. Butcher, my ass! I think you been cuttin' somebody!"

"Please, leave me alone."

"Is that whatchoo been doin'? You been cuttin' somebody? Who you been cuttin'? You got some money? Why don'tchoo give old Johnny Miller some money! Share some'a your wealth with us poor folk."

"I have no money. Please, leave me alone."

"You think your knife's bigger than my knife?"

Frenzy! Like being in a blender, like being in a cement mixer. "I asked you to leave me alone!"

"Don't matter how *big* it is. All that matters is how you use it, sucker!"

Whirling about in a cement mixer. Being poured out and set in place. *Frenzy!*

"This your car? Nice car. My cousin had a car like this, 'cept it was older. Lots older. What you got under that hood? A four-sixty? My cousin had a four-sixty, and it sure could haul ass. You got some money, then? You drive a car like this, you *got* to have money! Hey, I'm talkin' to you! *We're* talkin' to you! Me and my friend here—"

"I asked you to leave me alone."

"Jesus, Mary, and Joseph, yours *is* bigger than mine! But that don't matter. All that matters is how you—"

Two Weeks Later

"And what *I* want to know is," proclaimed Art Williamson, a paralegal who worked for the firm of Code, Boylan, Brown and Belcher, on the 96th floor of the Sears Tower, "how in the Sam hell can they really do an effective search of one million two hundred thousand three hundred and sixty four square feet of space in just two days? Which is exactly how much space we're talking about here. In this building. Which is, Janet,"—he was holding forth to a young and attractive legal assistant named Janet Weeks—"as you are no doubt aware the tallest building in the world. Bar none. Not even the World Trade Center is taller. We have, as a matter of fact, two more of the tallest buildings in the world here. In Chicago. Those buildings are the John Hancock Center, and the Standard Oil Building, which tops out at just a hair over one thousand, three hundred and twenty six feet. Of course, if you're talking about the CN Tower, in Toronto, that qualifies as the tallest *free-standing structure*—"

"What's that smell?" Janet cut in.

"In the world," Art finished, then asked, "What smell? I've got a cold."

Janet wrinkled her nose up. *"That* smell, for God's sake."

Art sniffed conspicuously, then shook his head. "I think you're imagining things, Janet. It's a not-uncommon phenomenon for women experiencing menstruation."

"Oh, Good Lord!"

"However, now that you mention it, there is a very slight odor. Sulfur, I'd say. Could be ozone. At this altitude, it's not uncommon."

Janet interrupted, nodding at an air-conditioning vent in the hallway ceiling above them. "It's coming from up there, I think."

Jack Whitehead was in his robe and slippers when he answered the knock at his front door. Two men in gray suits showed him badges and asked if they could come in.

"Sure, of course." Jack stepped away from the door. "Is this about Augusta? Have you found her?"

The taller of the two men, a homicide detective named Sam Gears, nodded grimly. "Yes, Mr. Whitehead, I believe we have."

Whitehead smiled. "That's wonderful. Where? When? Is she all right?"

"Perhaps you'd better sit down, sir," Gears said and nodded at a couch in Whitehead's living room.

Whitehead sat down abruptly. His smile vanished. He looked at the floor, shook his head, then looked up at Detective Gears. I don't believe it."

"Don't believe what, Mr. Whitehead?"

"That she's dead. She can't be dead. We were going to be married."

"No one said she was dead."

"Well, for Christ's sake, you didn't have me sit down here because it looked comfortable, did you?"

"No, sir."

Whitehead rose quickly, went into the kitchenette, poured some coffee, and glanced around at the two detectives. He held up the coffeepot. "Want some?" he asked.

"No, thanks," Gears answered. "Could you come downtown with us, sir? We need you to identify Miss Mullen's body."

"Identify her? No, I don't think so. But I'll tell you what: I'll describe her, instead. That'll make it easier for both of us. It'll save time, gas, aggravation. I don't like looking at dead bodies any more than you do." He paused, then continued, "So, she's five feet four inches tall, has short, dark-blond hair, a good figure—she always thought she was a little chunky . . ."

"We know you're upset, sir, but I'm afraid that we must insist."

There was a mirror-tiled wall opposite Whitehead's small dinette. He threw his cup of coffee at it—the cup shattered on the tiles and sprayed hot coffee and shards of porcelain far into the living area—then fell sobbing to his knees.

THE FOLLOWING DAY, AT THE EIGHTH PRECINCT

"You think there's a connection, don't you?" Detective George Ripley asked Gears.

"You don't?" Gears asked.

"Lots of people cut each other, Sam."

"I'm aware of that. But keep in mind that the lab said the wounds were made with similar instruments. And both murders happened on the same evening, within a few blocks of each other."

"Uh-huh. But the Mullen woman was wrapped in plastic and stuck up in the false ceiling. The other victim . . . what's his name?"

"Miller."

"Yeah. Miller. He was just . . . stuck." Ripley grinned.

Gears sipped a can of Diet Sprite, grimaced because it was warm, then dropped it in the wastebasket. "What have you got on those tire tracks?"

Ripley checked a computer printout on his desk. "Pirelli's. GR78–15s. A big, expensive tire, Sam, but there are several thousand of them in use in the county."

"And the plastic the Mullen woman was wrapped in?"

Ripley checked the same printout. "Twenty-gauge stuff. A polypropylene derivative . . . Painters use it, apparently. And car-repair shops. You can get it at fourteen or fifteen outlets in the city. My guess is that no one keeps records on who buys it, though."

"Look into it, anyway, George. It's possible this guy used a credit card, or a check—"

"You think he'd be that stupid, Sam?"

"We can live in hope."

TWO

They look like ants," a man said.

"It makes you feel so . . . insignificant, somehow," said his wife.

A young man nearby said, "If you dropped a penny from this high up, it would go right through someone's head."

"If it actually hit someone's head," said a young man with him. "The odds are pretty slim that it would even reach the street."

"Yeah," said the first young man, "and if you threw a paper airplane from up here, the chances are it would end up in the East River."

"It's the updrafts," said his friend.

"What's really neat," said the man with his wife, "is looking *up*. Go ahead, honey. Look up. It's like . . . looking into eternity."

"God, no," she said. "I have trouble enough looking *down*!"

INSIDE, ON THE 89TH FLOOR

Janet Dwyer had made plans to be married on July 14. She'd picked that date because it was the day, two years earlier, that she and her fiancé had met. She had been working as a volunteer for an organization distributing food to the needy. He was working as a fledgling reporter for the *Times* and was doing a story on the-plight-of-the-poverty-stricken-and-the-homeless-in-one-of-the-world's-largest-and-most-diverse-of-cities. She had liked him immediately because he cared so much about other people, and he had liked her, too, not only because she cared so much about other people, but because she was very good looking—in a girl-next-door kind of way—and had a quick, dry sense of humor.

Janet had counted on that sense of humor to carry her through the empty, harshly lit corridors and back to her office on the eighty-ninth floor, but it was failing her, and she wasn't sure why. Some new apprehension had all but snuffed it out.

She had never liked these corridors at night. They seemed unreal, as if she couldn't count on the walls staying put, or the floors holding her up. It was the altitude, she knew—the mere fact of how far she was from the ground. It gnawed at her sense of reality and security.

"Ever feel the building *sway* in the wind?" her co-worker, Sandy, was fond of asking.

"Oh, hell," her boss had assured her time and again, "the damned thing's built on bedrock, for God's sake. It'll be here for ten thousand years."

"But Manhattan's built on a swamp," she'd tell him, to which he could only sputter and wave her away.

Thirty feet ahead, the corridor branched to the left and right. The overhead lights were out where the corridors met, so the bright white fluorescents in the false ceiling above her caused very black, hard-edged shadows to form. These shadows in turn converged to form a V of light against the far wall; it gave the whole area a starkly symmetrical look. Janet thought that such hard, bright symmetry should not exist at a thousand feet above the ground, where the stars began. It was unreal; it was unnerving, as if she had stumbled upon another dimension.

Something moved where the corridors met. Janet stopped walking.

"Hello?" she called. "Who's there, please? Al"—the security guard—"is that you?" She got no reply. She took a deep, ragged breath. This, she decided, was the source of her new apprehension. This strange knowledge that something else was up here with her on the eighty-ninth floor. Something large and fast moving.

It appeared at the end of the corridor, within the harsh, bright V of light. Like a sprinting fullback, it moved nimbly and quickly toward her down the starkly lit corridor. It reached out. She heard something tear at her chest. She felt a moment of sharp, searing pain.

Then the corridor was empty.

She heard a deep choking sound. She saw the floor come up to her, felt her chin hit it, her nose. She turned over on her back, her arms wide. The choking sound continued, and she realized that it was coming from her own throat, and that blood was pooling around her, bright and red under the fluorescents.

She closed her eyes and murmured her pain and disbelief.

She felt hands on her. Felt herself being wrapped up in something smooth and cold. Then the air was gone and she was dead.

THREE

No," Ryerson Biergarten said to the chunky, round-faced man of twenty or so who sat down across from him. "I work alone. I'm sorry."

The young man, who had introduced himself as Lenny Baker, took a breadstick from a basket in the middle of the table and popped half of it into his mouth. He said as he chewed, "I don't need to tell you, Mr. Biergarten"—he paused, swallowed, went on—"hey, can I call you Rye? Is that all right?"

"Sure," Ryerson answered, though "Rye" was usually reserved only for his close friends.

"Thanks, Rye," Lenny said, smiling hugely, as if surprised. "I'll bet you're wondering how I knew some people called you that."

"No," Ryerson said, because *Rye* seemed to be an appropriate nickname for *Ryerson.*

"Well," said Lenny, "I'll tell you." He popped the rest of the breadstick into his mouth. "I'm psychic. Just like you."

"Oh?" Ryerson sipped his glass of ice water.

"For instance, I'll bet I know why you're in Toronto."

"That's public knowledge," Ryerson said.

Lenny looked crestfallen. "It is? How?"

"Through the newspapers," Ryerson answered. A waiter came over.

Lenny said, "Bring me a pasta salad, would you?" then turned questioningly to Ryerson. "And you, Rye? My treat."

Ryerson sighed. "Listen, Mr. Baker, I really don't mean to sound rude, but I've had a long and very tiring day."

"Call me Lenny. Please."

The waiter said to Ryerson, "A cocktail, sir?"

Lenny said, "Yes, a tutti-frutti."

"A tutti-frutti?" said the waiter.

"Sure, vodka, lemonade—"

"Sir," the waiter interrupted, addressing Ryerson now, "is that a dog at your feet?"

Ryerson looked down at Creosote, his Boston Bull terrier, who was curled up asleep near his right foot. He smiled apologetically at the waiter. "Yes," he said.

"Sir," said the waiter, "I don't know how you managed to get him in here, but I'm afraid that the sanitation laws do not permit—"

"But he's not *doing* anything," Ryerson protested.

"That's not the point, sir. The law clearly states—"

"Okay," Ryerson cut in, bent over, scooped up the sleeping Creosote, and stood. "Thanks, anyway." The waiter looked stunned. Ryerson looked at Lenny, said, "Have a good meal," and started for the door. After a moment, Lenny fell in behind him.

"The bastard," Lenny whispered.

Ryerson stopped and said firmly, "Please don't think you're going to be my shadow, Mr. Baker."

Lenny nodded enthusiastically at Creosote. "That's a Boston Bull terrier, isn't it? Ask me how I know."

Ryerson sighed.

"Because I'm psychic, just like you," Lenny said.

"Yes," Ryerson said, "you've told me that."

They were standing in the middle of the crowded restaurant. Another waiter came over, tapped Ryerson on the shoulder, and said, "Sir, I'm afraid we cannot allow dogs in this establishment."

"Oh, for Pete's sake!" Ryerson whispered.

"There," Lenny chirped. "I *knew* you were going to say that!"

Ryerson strode quickly to the exit, pulled on a door marked PUSH, murmured, "Oh, for Pete's sake!" again, pushed on the door, and left the restaurant.

It was raining.

Lenny was right at his heels.

"I've got an umbrella, Rye," he said.

Ryerson hailed a passing taxi, which kept going.

"Here," Lenny said, opened his umbrella, and held it over both of them.

Ryerson glanced at him and stepped out from under the umbrella. Lenny sidestepped to stay close to him. "You're going to get wet, Rye."

"I don't mind getting wet, Mr. Baker. I like it, in fact."

"No, you don't. Ask me how I know that."

Ryerson hailed another taxi, which pulled up to the curb. Ryerson yanked the rear door open and hopped in.

Lenny hopped in beside him, causing the taxi to lean.

The cabdriver looked back. "Yes, sir?"

Lenny said, "The Piddly-Widdly. It's on Bloor Street West."

Ryerson shook his head. "The Sheraton."

Lenny said, "They allow dogs at the Piddly Widdly. It's an outdoor café."

"And it's raining," Ryerson pointed out.

Lenny laughed. "I thought you were psychic, Rye. It's a *covered* outdoor café."

Very quickly, Ryerson reached to his left and opened the door. He gave Lenny a severe look. "Don't follow me," he growled, got out of the cab, and shut the door hard.

"Hey!" the cabbie protested. "Sorry," Ryerson said, and walked off toward the Sheraton Toronto. Behind him, he heard, "I'd be your Watson, Rye. He was overweight, at least the one in the movies was. So am I. And he wasn't too bright, either. Think about it, okay? I'm in the book."

Ryerson, soaked to the skin, was at the Sheraton Toronto a half-hour later.

The Next Day, in Downtown Toronto

Frenzy! Sometimes it was like seeing through someone else's eyes, as if what he was seeing wasn't real, as if it didn't matter, as if it were merely a movie being projected onto his corneas. That's when he knew he was in trouble. That's when he knew he'd wake up an hour later, twelve hours later, a day later, and wonder where he'd been, and what in the hell he'd done. And to whom.

"I'm possessed," he whispered. He had said it many, many times in the last eight years. Once he had even gone to a priest and begged for exorcism. The priest had merely shaken his head sadly and recommended that he get "professional help."

"But you *have* to do it," he had insisted. "It's your *job!*"

The priest shook his head again. He was in his sixties, graying at the temples, and was usually very paternal and capable looking. Now he looked as if he were being put upon. "I don't believe in possession, my son."

It was the last time he had gone to a priest.

He fumbled a bottle of scotch from his liquor cabinet, poured himself a shot, shook his head as if to clear it, and downed the scotch. He sensed that someone had come into the big room. He turned. "Yes, Roberta?" he whispered to the red-haired young woman in the doorway.

She said, "I thought I'd remind you of your three-thirty appointment." She paused, her brow furrowed. "Are you all right?"

He shook his head. "No." He turned, poured another shot of scotch. "No," he repeated and downed the scotch. "I'm tired." He looked at her. "Is there any way I can get out of that appointment?"

"It's with the people from the zoning commission. We've already asked for three postponements."

"Dammit to hell!" he whispered.

"Sorry," said the red-haired woman, surprised, because he rarely cursed. "Are you sure you're all right?"

"I didn't *say* I was all right, Roberta. I *said* I wasn't feeling well."

"Oh." His anger surprised her. She had worked with him for ten months now and had never seen him angry before. "Yes, of course." She started backing out of the room. "Three-thirty—that's in a half-hour."

"I can read a clock, goddammit!"

"Yes, sir." She left quickly.

She knocked on the door twenty minutes later, called his name, got no answer, opened the door, and stuck her head in. She called to him again, thinking he was in the bathroom which adjoined his cavernous office. "Ten minutes," she said. Still she got no answer. She went into the room, called to him again, saw that the bathroom door was open and that the bathroom was empty.

She pursed her lips. "Great!" she whispered.

He was nowhere in sight.

Ryerson Biergarten had very little to tell Homicide Detective Dan Creed, and Creed knew it as soon as Ryerson came into his glass-enclosed office. He said, "Nothing, right?"

Ryerson closed the door, nodded glumly, and sat down in front of Creed's desk. "It happens that way sometimes, Dan. Not very often, but sometimes. I'm sorry." He put Creosote on the floor and said, "Stay!" The little dog looked confused, then curled up at Ryerson's feet.

Detective Creed, a square-faced, heavily built, competent-looking man in his early forties, said, "It was a long shot, anyway. The kid will turn up sooner or later."

Ryerson shook his head. "I don't think so, Dan." He

gave Creed a flat, apologetic smile. "At least I can tell you that much. I don't think anyone will see Martin Cobb, alive or dead, ever again."

Creed said, "I hope you're wrong, Rye." He nodded at a file folder lying open on his desk. "So, the case is closed as far as you're concerned? I can have accounting draw up a check for you."

Ryerson hesitated, leaned forward, turned the file around, and scanned the relevant data on the missing boy, although he had memorized most of it.

He leaned back. "Give me another day on this, okay, Dan? No charge."

Creed grinned. "Professional pride?"

Ryerson nodded. "That's part of it, yes." He paused, heard a strange, low crunching sound whose source he couldn't pinpoint, and went on, "It's one of the 'sins that flesh is heir to,' isn't it? Pride." The crunching sound grew louder, more enthusiastic. Ryerson continued, "I don't like coming up against a stone wall. No one does. And I really would like to find this boy."

"I can't blame you for that," Creed said.

Ryerson nodded at the file. "Do you mind if I take that with me, Dan? Maybe I overlooked something. Maybe there's a piece of physical evidence, a location—"

Creed broke in, "What the hell is that noise?"

Ryerson looked down at Creosote. The dog had one leg of Creed's desk firmly between his teeth; he had already gnawed half the leg into oblivion. Ryerson scooped him up and shook a finger at him. "No. Bad dog!" He looked apologetically at Creed. "I'm sorry, Dan."

Creed smiled. "Does he still go after your socks, Rye?"

Ryerson sighed. "Every chance he gets." He felt Creosote licking his chin. "Take the cost of repairing the desk off my check, okay, Dan?"

Creed said, "He's ugly, but he's got character, I'll say that for him. Don't worry about the desk." He handed the file to Ryerson. "And if you think you can get something more out of this, be my guest."

Frenzy!

Like being in a cement mixer.

"Hey, you okay, buddy?"

"My head hurts. I'll be all right."

"You don't look all right. You want to go to the hospital? I could take you to the hospital. No charge."

"Thank you. I'll be all right."

"It's just a couple minutes from here—"

"I said I'll be all right, goddammit!"

"Suit yourself. Just trying to help."

And so the rain. Hadn't it been raining forever? Wasn't he soaked to the skin, to the bone, the marrow?

Wasn't he floating in it?

Wasn't he floating? Didn't his hair billow out clean, and couldn't he propel himself? Like a fish?

Couldn't he move as fast as light?

Didn't he carry judgment with him, and power!

Couldn't he dance, and didn't the sweet, surging updrafts push his hair about? Didn't he float? Wasn't he held up by the updrafts?

Couldn't he dance on the updrafts? Wasn't he nimble? Didn't he carry judgment and power on either hand?

Yes! Oh, yes!

FOUR

When Ryerson had started work on the Martin Cobb disappearance a week and a half earlier, he had gotten several of Martin's personal effects from the boy's mother, a widow who lived in the prestigious north end of Toronto. These items included a small spiral notebook that Martin had filled with adolescent poetry, a Revell model 1932 Buick Roadster with one headlight missing, a white T-shirt that had "GIZMO" emblazoned on it in red, a battered black-and-white Nike sneaker minus its shoelace, and a dog-eared paperback copy of *The Time Machine*—"Martin just loves that kind of stuff, Mr. Biergarten," his mother had said.

Ryerson had spread all these items out on the bed in his hotel room and had been touching each one lightly with his fingertips. It was something he had done several times in the past week and a half, and though he had no trouble getting psychic images from each item, the meaning of those images had eluded him, even when he asked Martin's mother about them.

"I touch the paperback book, Mrs. Cobb, and I get the image of a . . . hot dog." He paused, embarrassed, though he wasn't sure why. "A red-hot," he explained.

She shrugged. "I've never read the book, of course, Mr. Biergarten."

"And when I touch the sneaker, all I get is—pardon me, please—is someone's . . . derriere. It's moving. It's a girl's . . . derriere, and it's moving. Did Martin have a girlfriend?"

That had offended Mrs. Cobb. "No, of course not. Martin was only fourteen years old, after all. What right-thinking fourteen-year-old is concerned with girls, Mr. Biergarten? I would say they have other things to be concerned with, wouldn't you? Baseball, for instance, and . . . and other *boyish* things."

"Yes, of course. I'm sorry." A pause. "And when I touch the notebook, all I get is the sound of someone weeping distantly."

Mrs. Cobb had pursed her lips. "That notebook was his undoing, if you ask me, Mr. Biergarten. He spent far too much time with it. Poetry, indeed! If his father were alive, he wouldn't have allowed it. Weeping, you say? That would have to be *me,* wouldn't it? *Me* weeping for his weakness and his . . . his sensi*tiv*ity!"

That session with her had gone very badly. If the images Ryerson had gotten from Martin's personal effects had been conflicting and nebulous, the images he'd gotten from Mrs. Cobb had been only too concrete: resentment, frustration, grief. And fear. Ryerson sensed that without her son or her husband, Mrs. Cobb's future seemed filled with loneliness and uncertainty.

* * *

Now, alone in his hotel room—Martin's personal effects spread out on the bed—Ryerson got precisely the same images he had gotten then: a hot dog, some anonymous, bouncing rear end, and the distant sound of weeping, which was obviously a deep inner sadness that Martin disguised none too well in his poetry.

Ryerson picked up the spiral notebook, flipped to the middle, read the poem there aloud:

> "Oh, ant, oh, ant, there in the ground,
> When you walk, there is no sound,
> When you breathe, there is no breath,
> When you die, there is no death!
> Oh, ant, oh, ant, in the ground I see,
> How I wish I were like thee!"

Ryerson set the notebook down and whispered, "You're a troubled young man, aren't you, Martin?"

Yes, he heard.

Ryerson fell silent.

Yes! he heard again, louder, more urgently. *Yes! Yes!*

"Martin?"

Yes! he heard again.

"Martin Cobb?"

Help me! Help me, please!

"Martin, where are you?"

Yes, yes, yes!

"Please tell me where you are!"

Come to the house. Oh, come to the house!

* * *

An hour later, Ryerson pressed Mrs. Cobb: "A country house, then, if not a beach house."

"No, of course not. *This* is the only house we have." She paused. "Except for the summer house, of course. But that's been shut up for years. I doubt that Martin even remembers it."

"A summer house? Where?"

She shook her head. "He couldn't have known about it, Mr. Biergarten. He just couldn't have. He hasn't been in it for ten years. His father died there."

"Please, Mrs. Cobb, where *is* it?"

She sighed. "Fifty miles north, near a village called Lakeville."

"Dan, this is Rye. I'm at Mrs. Cobb's house and I think I'm on to something. Have you heard of a village called Lakeville?"

"Yes, I have," Creed answered. "Why?"

"I think Martin's there."

A brief silence, then, "I'll pick you up. Give me a half hour." A dial tone followed.

Ryerson hung up and turned to Mrs. Cobb, who was standing behind him with a look of hopeful anticipation on her face. "Did I hear you correctly, Mr. Biergarten? Do you really think you've found Martin?"

"Yes," Ryerson answered. "I think he's alive." The words made him uncomfortable, and he wasn't sure why. Perhaps it was his professional skepticism, which should have made him cautiously optimistic, at best. But he was certain of what he had heard. Certain of its source, certain of its reality. To waffle, now, in front of this poor, tormented woman, would be cruel. Of *course* Martin was alive. He was at the summer house in Lakeville and he was alive!

It was a three-story, blue-green, wood-shingled house near the center of a small stand of pine trees. There were many small, narrow windows set starkly against the massive bulk of the house.

Because it had been empty for almost a decade, Ryerson had supposed that the house would have a pronounced look of decay and abandonment about it. But it didn't, and this confused him.

He said to Mrs. Cobb, who was walking between him and Inspector Creed up the pine-needle-covered brick walkway to the house, "Does someone live here?"

"No," she answered.

"I don't understand," Ryerson said. "Didn't you tell me that it's been empty—"

"Yes. It has. I keep it up because John likes it that way, Mr. Biergarten. It's been repainted twice. The roof has been replaced. And a housekeeper comes in once a week to do whatever cleaning is necessary." They were on the wide wraparound porch now. Mrs. Cobb fished in her purse for a few seconds, found a key ring, and put one of the keys in the lock. She looked pleadingly at Ryerson. "It's painful for me to be here, Mr. Biergarten."

"Yes, I understand that."

"I was last here shortly after John died. I was going to sell the place, but of course John told me not to. He said,

'Where would I go?' " She turned the key in the lock. "I had no answer for him. I told him that he couldn't come back to Toronto." She pushed on the door.

Creed began, "Are you telling us, Mrs. Cobb, that you believe that you actually spoke with—"

Ryerson put his hand on Creed's arm and cut in, "Of course she spoke with her husband, Dan."

"Of course," said Mrs. Cobb, looking surprised. "And so he stays here. All by himself. Except for the house-keeper, and I'd say she doesn't know a thing about him." She pushed the door open.

Ryerson was about to ask whether he could be alone in the house for a few minutes, but when he looked through the small foyer and into the large living room beyond, he murmured, "My God," instead, and stepped quickly into the house. Mrs. Cobb followed. She smiled pleasantly, as a hostess would.

Inspector Creed said, "What is it, Rye?"

Ryerson stopped at the end of the foyer, where it opened onto the living room. "Someone's been living here," he said.

Mrs. Cobb said, "Yes. John has been living here."

The heavily furnished living room bore the unmistak-able look of having been lived in. The cushions on the big green corduroy couch had slight indentations in them; books in the three large bookcases against one wall were askew; a copy of *Popular Mechanics* lay open on a side table. A floor lamp was switched on.

Creed said to Mrs. Cobb, "You've kept the electricity hooked up all these years?"

"Of course," she answered, and settled into a big green

corduroy chair. "For John's sake. And so the furnace will work in the winter, so the pipes won't burst, and the paint won't peel, and the walls won't crack."

Ryerson realized that he was hearing a different woman from the one he'd been dealing with in the past ten days. He was hearing a bizarre kind of pragmatist, someone who believed without question in the ghost of her long-dead husband and wanted to make his afterlife, in the house where he died, as comfortable as possible. But a woman who wanted, also, to protect the ceiling joists from dry rot, the cellar from slow leaks, and the hardwood floors from mildew.

She said, "John's always been an untidy man."

"Your son is here," Ryerson said to her.

"No," she corrected, "John's here."

Ryerson glanced at Inspector Creed, who looked very ill at ease, then back at Mrs. Cobb. He extended his hand. "I'm going to search the house, Mrs. Cobb. I'd like you to come with me."

She looked questioningly at his hand, at Inspector Creed, then at Ryerson's hand again. She smiled a flat, odd smile, said, "Yes, of course," took his hand, and rose. "It's a very big house." She looked at Inspector Creed and said, "It's a very big house, Inspector, and if Martin is hiding in it . . ." She stopped. Her smile vanished. Suddenly she looked confused, as if unsure of where she was. She shook her head and looked accusingly at Ryerson. "Why have you brought me here?"

Ryerson squeezed her hand. "I believe that Martin is here, Mrs. Cobb. I *know* that he's here. I . . ." He paused very briefly. He didn't want to say what he was about to say, but the words were already piling up at the back of his tongue. They spilled out. "I spoke with him."

Creed said, "You *spoke* with him? You never told me that. You told me you got *impressions!*"

Mrs. Cobb's mouth opened, then closed. "Yes?" she whispered anxiously. "And what did he say?"

Creed broke in, "What do you mean you spoke with him? Christ, Rye, that's a hell of a long way from . . . getting *impressions,* isn't it?"

"It happens, Dan."

Creed shook his head. "No, it doesn't. You've taken me for a ride, my friend—"

"Dan, please, I know what I'm doing."

Creed shook his head again. "They warned me about hiring you. They made jokes about it. They asked me where I kept my crystal ball—no, that's not what they asked me, they asked me if I *had* crystal balls!"

"Dan, you're not being fair."

Mrs. Cobb broke in, "Yes, I can feel it, too. Martin really *is* here!" She started walking toward the stairway which led to the second floor. "He really *is* here!" she whispered.

And from above came a series of quick, low thudding noises.

FIVE

As he moved swiftly up the stairway with Mrs. Cobb and Inspector Creed behind him, Ryerson heard distantly, "Shit, oh, shit!" It was the voice of a young man.

"Let me through!" Creed ordered.

Ryerson glanced at him. Creed had his gun drawn. "You don't need that, Dan!"

"Just let me through!" He pushed past Ryerson, onto the landing, stopped, and bellowed down the long, unlighted hallway, "I'm a police officer. Show yourself!"

"Put the gun away, Dan," Ryerson pleaded. "You don't need it."

Creed ignored him. He repeated, "I'm a police officer. Show yourself!"

Mrs. Cobb brushed past Ryerson and Creed and started down the hallway. "Martin?" she called. "It's mommy. Don't be afraid."

"Mrs. Cobb," Creed snapped, "for God's sake!"

She bolted.

Ryerson heard again, "Shit, oh, shit!" and realized that, as before, he hadn't heard the words—though they were real enough—so much as sensed them. The words were tiny whispers of desperation—*I've been caught!* they said.

Mrs. Cobb disappeared into a room on the left side of the hallway. Creed went after her, his gun still drawn. Ryerson went after Creed. He had a sinking feeling in his gut, now. He followed Creed into the room Mrs. Cobb had gone into. The overhead light was on. Mrs. Cobb stood in the center of the room with her head cocked and her gaze on a dark-haired, square-faced, frightened-looking man huddled between a chest of drawers and a closet door. The man was in his early twenties, Ryerson guessed. He was dressed in faded jeans and a rumpled white shirt whose sleeves were rolled up to mid-forearm. There were what looked like grass stains at the elbows of the shirt. The man was barefooted.

Mrs. Cobb said, "What are you doing here?"

The man whimpered, "I didn't mean nothin'. She said I could stay here."

Creed put his gun back in its shoulder holster. "Who said you could stay here?"

"She did," the young man answered. "The house keeper did."

"Her name is Flora Babbet," Mrs. Cobb explained.

"Oh," Creed said.

Ryerson took several steps backward, as if distancing himself from what was happening in the room. He said nothing. Humiliation was flooding through him like a sudden onslaught of nausea. This young man's high, pleading whimper was what he had heard in his hotel room—not Martin Cobb's plea for help, but this young man's pleading, diseased whimper.

Creed ordered, "Get up out of there."

The young man shook his head dismally.

Mrs. Cobb said, "Do you know John?"

Again the young man shook his head, but then he began to stand shakily, as if his legs were weak. Ryerson sensed illness in him, something chronic and debilitating. Tuberculosis, maybe. He said, his voice low, "This young man is sick."

Creed crossed the room, took the young man by the elbow, and pulled him to his feet. The young man coughed low and deep in his chest.

"Tuberculosis," Ryerson said.

"Do you know John?" Mrs. Cobb asked again.

The young man looked confused, alone, dismal. "I don't know no John," he managed. Then, to Creed and Ryerson, "That woman's nuts." He coughed again, deeply, gurglingly, spittle arching from his lips. Creed, who was still holding his arm, grimaced. "That woman's nuts," the young man repeated.

"Do you know John?" Mrs. Cobb asked again. "And Martin?" she added, almost as an afterthought. Her words were high and strained, like a balloon whose air is being slowly released.

The young man looked suddenly frightened. "No," he said. He shook his head, then began coughing again. This time it caught up with him. He managed several more "nos" while coughing, then lost his breath and crumpled, wheezing, to the floor. He pitched forward to all fours, still wheezing. Then his arms buckled and he lay face-down, quiet.

Ryerson bent over him. "Hell," he whispered. He looked at Mrs. Cobb. "Is the phone hooked up?"

"Why would the phone be hooked up?" she answered.

Ryerson turned the young man over. His skin was a deep blue. "He's not getting any air."

Inspector Creed said, "I know CPR."

Ryerson shook his head. "I don't think it's necessary." He paused. The young man's color was returning. "We've got to get him to a hospital."

Mrs. Cobb was astonished. "But what about Martin?"

Ryerson sighed. "I'm sorry. I was wrong." He looked at Creed. "Give me a hand, would you?" Together, they lifted the young man and started out of the room with him.

"No, you weren't wrong," Mrs. Cobb announced desperately behind them. "You were right. He's here. I know it!"

Ryerson glanced back at her as he rounded the bedroom doorway into the corridor. She had a look of fear and pleading on her face. She looked as alone, as hurt, as dismal as the young man had. "I'm sorry, Mrs. Cobb," he said. "I'm really very sorry."

SIX

H e said, "But the article in the newspaper—"
The old priest interrupted, "Was mostly hype, I'm
afraid. It sells papers, but it's hype, it's crap. I do
not *do* exorcisms, I do not *perform* them—it is not a
media event that I am involved in. It is not something for
show. I *persuade.*"

He was confused. "But isn't that the same thing,
really?"

The old priest shook his head. "I wish it were. I really
wish that exorcism involved devils and demons and possession in the way that the movies depict it. But what it
involves, I'm afraid, is something much more mundane.
It involves *disturbance,* and *illness.* I exorcise the demons
that people produce within themselves, my son. There
are no other demons than those."

He shook his head. "You're wrong."

"Obsessive-compulsive," said the old priest. "You've
heard the term, of course."

He merely sighed.

"Everyone's heard it," said the old priest. "This is the
age of psychobabble." He smiled slyly. "Someone's

doing something he shouldn't, someone's got some nasty habit he can't break, and his friends say, 'Oh, he's exhibiting obsessive-compulsive behavior.' And they say it as if they know what it means. They don't. They can't. Just as a dog can't know what it means to be a fish, people who"—he formed quotes with his fingers—"'have it all together' can't know what it means to be totally incapable of controlling their actions. As if some outside force is maneuvering them. As if they've relegated control of themselves to someone or some*thing* else."

"Precisely!" he said.

"Bullshit!" declared the old priest.

Ryerson thought that it wasn't the first time he had fouled up. He shook his head. *Fouled up* was too kind, too friendly, too forgiving. He'd *failed,* and through his failure, through his pride, he had brought grief to another human being.

Martin Cobb was dead and gone. Ryerson knew it. He felt it. He had known it and felt it ever since he'd come to Toronto. So, if there was a reason for what he—Ryerson—had done, that reason was hope. Mrs. Cobb needed hope, and he had given it to her.

"That's a rationalization, Biergarten," he whispered. What he had given her was false hope, and in this world there was probably nothing worse. It made the inevitable onslaught of grief overwhelming. It made people crumble.

Mrs. Cobb had crumbled finally, after the young man who had invaded her summer house had died. "Tuberculosis, yes," the attending physician confirmed. "And diabetes, which is what killed him. Insulin coma."

She had collapsed, then. She had been taken away on a stretcher and now was recovering in the psychiatric wing of Queen's Hospital. "She'll be all right," the doctor had said. "It's the end of an ordeal for her. She saw this young man's death apparently as confirmation, in a way, that her own son will not be coming back to her. And while that may or may not be literally true, she *perceives* that it is true, and it's as if a great weight has been lifted from her."

Ryerson knew well enough what the doctor had been saying, but as far as Mrs. Cobb was concerned, he thought, it may have been only half the story. Her grief had been too intense. He had felt it rising from her like waves of fever.

But still she would recover. She would carry on with her life, and at times would find herself lost in the memory of her son, and would become mired in the memory of the psychic detective who had misled her.

Ryerson sighed. This—his handling of the Cobb disappearance—was one of those blessedly rare events in life that he would look forward to putting far, far behind him. Five years from now, he would say to himself, *It was five years ago that I did that. Not long enough.* And ten years later, he would say, *It was fifteen years ago that I did that. The memory's beginning to fade.*

On the other side of the hotel room, Creosote growled low in his chest. Ryerson glanced at him. "Oh, for Pete's sake!" he whispered. Somehow, the dog had gotten one of Ryerson's argyle socks and was noisily reducing it to mush. Ryerson slammed shut the lid of the suitcase he'd been packing, vaulted across the room, and scooped Creosote into his arms. For several seconds they stared at each other—man condemningly at dog, dog confusedly at man. The shredded argyle sock was still in Creosote's mouth. Ryerson pointed his index finger stiffly into the air near Creosote's nose. "No!" he bellowed. "Bad dog!"

Creosote gurgled. Like all Boston Bull terriers, he was asthmatic, so he gurgled and wheezed quite a lot. Usually, a gurgle or a wheeze from that flat, gummy, toothy face was unpleasant, at best. However, Ryerson was able to read something that might have been apology in this particular gurgle, or something that was as close to an apology as a Boston Bull terrier can get.

So, Ryerson apologized. What was an argyle sock between friends, after all? Let Creosote have it. "Sorry, pal," he said and carried Creosote back to the corner of the room and set him down. Creosote immediately dropped the argyle sock and trotted into the bathroom. The tile floor near the toilet had become his favorite spot for a surreptitious pee. Ryerson ran after him. "No," he yelled, "bad dog. Bad dog!" But when he got there, the deed was already underway.

On the fifty-sixth floor of the Commerce Court West Building, Inspector Creed was bent over the corpse of a man in his late fifties who was dressed in green work pants and shirt, white socks, and black shoes. The corpse had fallen through the false ceiling an hour earlier, narrowly missing a young file clerk. It was wrapped in heavy-gauge clear plastic; blue wire as thick as a coat hanger was tied, outside the plastic, around its chest and thighs. "We think it's the janitor," Creed had been told by Detective Max Tyler.

Creed carefully pulled the plastic away from the corpse's face. He noted the large nose, the flat, open eyes, the thin white, slightly parted lips, the chipped gray teeth. He let his gaze follow the length of the body itself. "Big man," he said.

Tyler, standing near the foot of the corpse, said, "Two-fifty, anyway. He was wired to the sprinkler system. The wires unwound and he fell. Jesus, whoever put him up there had to have been awfully damned strong." He paused. "Maybe two people did it."

"Maybe," Creed said. He noted the football-size mass of coagulated blood at the corpse's belly. "If he'd been murdered up here, this hallway would be a godawful mess."

"We're looking," Tyler said.

"Yeah, well, don't look too long." He nodded at the ends of wire jutting raggedly toward the ceiling. "That wire would have held him up there forever if it had been tied right."

"Maybe our killer *wanted* him to fall," Tyler shrugged. "Maybe he hoped someone would be underneath." He nodded at a slightly built woman in her early twenties; the woman had short dark hair and wore big, owlish glasses perched halfway down her small nose. She was standing at the end of the corridor, where it branched to the left and right, and she was shaking visibly. A police matron stood with her, arm comfortingly around her shoulders. Tyler continued, "Her name's Connie Bee-chum. She works in the building. She said when this guy fell she thought it was an earthquake and the building was coming apart and people were starting to fall through from above." He smiled. "It sure would have scared the bejesus out of me—I can tell you that." He nodded at the corpse. "Then she saw the plastic, and the wire"—he shrugged—"and here we are, trying to make sense of it."

Creed asked, "Has someone gotten a statement from her?"

Tyler nodded, "Yeah, Dan. I have."

"Then why is she still here?"

Tyler shrugged. "Beats the crap out of me, Dan. Do you want me to find out?"

Creed gave him a flat, impatient smile. "Why don't you do that, Max."

Tyler shrugged again. He shrugged quite a lot; it was a habit that Creed found annoying. "Whatever you say, Dan. Hell, maybe she just likes to look at dead bodies." He grinned, then went to talk to Connie Beechum.

Creed looked up through the jagged hole in the false ceiling. The plumbing for the sprinkler system was bent from the weight of the body. At two points, the green pipe had been stripped of paint by the wire that had held up the body. Creed shook his head. God, but this was one for the books. If there turned out to be a parallel anywhere, he'd be very surprised.

Tyler reappeared. Connie Beechum was with him, still shaking visibly. Tyler said, "Miss Beechum has some-thing else she wants to tell us, Dan."

Creed shook her hand. It was cold and moist. "I'm sorry for your ordeal here, Miss Beechum."

She smiled quiveringly. "I thought it was an earthquake."

"Yes," Creed said. "Thank God it wasn't." He took her arm and walked her a dozen feet down the corridor. Tyler fell in behind them.

Creed asked, "There was something else, Miss Beechum?"

She adjusted her glasses, which had slid down to the tip of her nose, and gave him another quivering smile. "Yes," she whispered, cleared her throat and said, in a voice that was high-pitched nearly to the point of squeakiness, "A man."

"A man?" Creed coaxed.

She nodded. Again her glasses slid down her nose. She adjusted them. "A man," she repeated.

"Perhaps you could elaborate," Creed said.

"Yes, I think so." She was clearly straining to remember. "It was several days ago. Three days ago, anyway. Friday, I think. Yes, it was Friday—I remember I had my paycheck with me." She smiled, happy that she was beginning to remember. "And I was going to lunch. No, wait. I'd had lunch. Yes. I remember. I was going . . . back to my office." She stopped, looked embarrassed, and went on, "No, that's not true. I was going to the ladies' room on forty-eight."

"The forty-eighth floor?"

"Yes. And I saw a man." She stopped.

"You mean you saw a man in the ladies' room?"

She shook her head quickly. "No, of course not. I

would have reported *that* at once. No. He was walking
past it."

"And?"

"And I didn't recognize him. I've worked in this building for three years, and I have a very good memory for
faces."

"Of course."

"And I didn't remember his." She smiled broadly. "I
thought I should tell you."

"Could you describe him?"

"Yes, I can describe him. He was very executive-
looking."

"Executive-looking?"

"A management type. He had a paunch. He had exploded surface capillaries on his face from too much
drinking. His hair didn't move."

"His hair didn't move?"

"That's right. He was walking very quickly. He was
almost running. And his hair didn't move. He had short,
thinning, management-length brown hair. It didn't *say*
anything at all—it wasn't too short; it wasn't too long; it
was simply there. Hair is not supposed to be important
to management types, so they spend a lot of time making
sure it's not noticeable. One way to do that is to be
certain it's not going to move."

"Yes." Creed smiled a little. "And how old would you
say he was, Miss Beechum?"

"How old? He was management age, naturally. That is
to say, he appeared to be no particular age between
thirty-eight and fifty-two or fifty-three. My guess would
be that he was forty-five. But that is only a guess. It's

accurate, I'd say, to within minus seven and plus eight years."

"Which means," said Creed, realizing that he was getting precious little from her, "that he could have been between thirty-eight and fifty-three."

"Yes. But he was probably forty-five." She glanced at the corpse. Technicians had arrived and were dusting the plastic for fingerprints. "He," she said, "is a blue-collar type." She pursed her lips. "At least he was."

Creed said, "Could you tell us what the man you saw was wearing?"

She nodded. "Gray."

"You mean he was wearing a gray suit?"

"Yes. And black shoes. Wing tips. They were scuffed, especially at the toe, so he wasn't a high-management-level executive."

"Oh?"

She smiled, pleased to get a chance to explain. "He stretches his legs out under his desk, and the toes of his shoes hit the front of the desk. So he has a smallish desk. High-management-level executives have very large desks, which they are hardly ever behind, anyway."

Creed grinned. A budding Sherlock Holmes, he thought. "Of course," he said.

"It's very logical, inspector."

One of the technicians came over. "We're going to take the plastic off the body now."

"Thanks," Creed said. "I'll be right there."

Connie Beechum said, "I'd like to watch, if it's all right."

SEVEN

Creed handed Ryerson a check. "I'm afraid we had to deduct for the trip to Lakeville, Rye. Sorry."

"No problem," Ryerson put the check into his coat pocket without looking at it. He cocked his head.

After a few moments of silence, Creed said, "Is something wrong?"

Ryerson cocked his head the other way.

"You're getting spooky," Creed said.

"Polypropylene," Ryerson whispered.

"Sorry?"

"Cocoon," Ryerson said.

"Yes, I've seen it."

Creed looked at him a few moments. Ryerson stayed quiet. Creed barked, "For Christ's sake, what in the hell are you staring at?"

Ryerson cocked his head the other way.

Creed fumed, "Will you say something, dammit?!"

"Plastic," Ryerson whispered.

Creed hesitated only a moment, then, "Oh, get the hell out of here!"

"He was wrapped in plastic," Ryerson said aloud, as if to himself.

"Yeah," said Creed, "and he had a birthday candle stuck in his belly. I don't know what you're babbling about."

"I can dance," Ryerson whispered, his voice suddenly very low and harsh.

Creed jumped up, came quickly around the desk, took Ryerson by the arm and lifted him from his chair. "Get the hell out of my office!" He shoved him toward the door. Ryerson stumbled, put his hand on the door jamb, lowered his head. "I can dance," he repeated. "I have power."

Creed reached around him, pulled the door open, and shoved him out into the squad room. "Billings?" he called to a burly uniformed officer nearby. Billings came over.

"Escort this man from the building," Creed ordered.

Late that evening, several miles north of Hamilton, Ontario, on his way back to Boston in his yellow Volkswagen Super Beetle, Ryerson pulled onto the shoulder of the road. A hundred feet ahead, up out of the reach of the headlights, a lighted billboard advertised a local McDonald's. On the ground beneath it, two deer watched him. Ryerson, whose night vision was dismal at best, saw the deer only as two pair of bright blue eyes, one pair slightly higher than the other, and two whitish, dully rectangular forms beneath. He knew that they were deer because he could sense a sharp tension in them that quivered on the edge of panic. Soon, he knew, they would bolt. For now, their eyes were a point of focus.

He had known all day that he'd had a kind of blackout in Creed's office, but the details had remained sketchy. He remembered only the word "birthplace," the smell of cheap after-shave and sweat, remembered being on the street, the stares of the passersby.

The blackout was a phenomenon he had experienced before, especially if the impressions he received were strong. These impressions had been very strong, as if he had suddenly been encased in someone else's skin, had been using someone else's brain, memory, needs, and passions.

But now, his gaze on the bright blue eyes of the deer, he remembered more. Much more.

He remembered being able to fly.

He remembered speed, agility, strength, freedom. And power.

The deer bolted. A car passing Ryerson screeched to a halt to avoid them. The second deer froze. The bumper of the car clipped the deer's hind leg, and a scorching pain shot through Ryerson. He stiffened. The pain dissipated. The deer sprang across the road, apparently unhurt, and was gone.

Ryerson closed his eyes. "My God!" he whispered. On the backseat, Creosote whimpered in his sleep.

Ryerson put the Beetle in gear and made a U-turn. He was going back to Toronto.

In Toronto, the hangers-on at a late-night cocktail party had turned with enthusiasm to giddy, near-drunken talk about death and dying. There were four men and two women, and it was a remark by one of the women that had sparked the conversation. At the age of forty-eight, Milly Farino, a sometime candidate for various political offices in Toronto, had lost three husbands to divorce, one to a heart attack, and another in a freak plane crash. Everyone jumped on her remark, "Death is the great equalizer," because it was short, catchy, and undeniably true.

"Ashes to ashes and dust to dust," slurred financial analyst Thomas Payton from his club chair. "All dust is equal, eh?" he added. It was, he decided, one of his most quotable remarks.

"This," said Jackson Lord, seated in another club chair not far from Payton's—there were several empty glasses on the floor near his chair, and a nearly full glass of Canadian whiskey in his hand—"is what death is all about: Death"—he took a long pull on his whiskey—"is the end of a good time."

"That's pretty basic, isn't it?" asked Gloria O'Malley, a tall, willowy, oval-faced, high-cheekboned brunette dressed in a shiny, sequin-studded black gown. The gown had somehow gotten ripped at her right hip, revealing lots of snow-white skin beneath. "I mean, it's almost cynical."

"Logical," countered Jackson Lord.

"Well, I don't think we're being philosophical enough about this whole thing," said Maurice L'Oreal, a visitor from Quebec.

"What's philosophical about death?" asked Payton. "It *is*. It happens. There's nothing philosophical about it." He felt again that he had uttered the profundity of the evening. "You might as well try to get philosophical about . . . tile grout."

"About *what*?" asked Gloria O'Malley, smiling very broadly and toothily.

"Why the hell are we talking about it?" asked a man in a gray suit.

"Because death is a good topic, Rick," Professor Lincoln Curtsinger said. "It's the only topic, really. Besides life."

"That's the spirit," toasted Jackson Lord.

"It stinks," said the man in the gray suit.

"You watch out there, Rick," teased Maurice L'Oreal. "That's a value judgment."

"Death stinks," Rick repeated. "So does talking about it."

Milly Farino, sensing the grim mood settling in, said, "I'm sorry I brought it up. We can talk about something else. Let's talk about politics. That's a good topic, too."

"Death stinks," Rick said again.

"You're stuck, my friend," said Maurice L'Oreal. "Death doesn't stink, you see. It *is*, simply. *Is*. Tile grout stinks." He laughed.

"I suffocated a puppy once," said Anson Wyler, bringing the conversation to a nasty halt.

"You *what*?" Milly Farino whispered.

"I had to," Wyler explained. "It was in pain. It really was in tremendous pain." He was pleading with them. "It was very weak, and it was in a lot of pain, and I had a decision to make." He took a sip of his drink, coughed. "So I suffocated it. I put a plastic bag over its head, and

I put my hand around its throat. Hard. Very hard. Not as hard as I could, but hard enough. And it died." Another nervous sip of his drink. "Eventually."

"Eventually?"

He nodded. "It took a long, long time. Christ, it took a hell of a lot longer than I thought it would. I was screaming at it. 'For God's sake, die. Please die!'" He stopped, clearly embarrassed.

Rick said, "You did it wrong. That's why it took as long as it did. You prolonged its suffering. But of course you know that."

And, of course, Anson did know it. He had known it forever. "You can't plan something like that, Rick," he explained dismally.

"No," said Rick, "not something like that. I know." He sipped his ginger ale, his drink of choice and necessity. "You can plan other things."

"What other things?" asked Milly.

Rick nodded. He had been standing all the while. Now he sat on the couch next to Gloria O'Malley, who grimaced a little. He was a heavyset man, and when he sat, he spilled some of his ginger ale onto his black pants. "Death," he explained. "You can plan the quickness of it."

"Are you talking about suicide?" Milly asked.

"I could be." Rick's words were slow and thoughtful. "You can plan the quickness of your own suicide. No one who chooses suicide chooses something slow and agonizing. Suicides want to exit life quickly, instantaneously, though that's not possible, of course. Nothing is instantaneous. The word itself is a misnomer. If anything were actually 'instantaneous,' per se, then time would not exist. And, of course, time *does* exist. We're all swimming in it." He leaned forward, set his glass on the floor between his feet, put his elbows on his knees, clenched his hands, and smiled a flat, humorless smile. "We're all dancing in time," he whispered.

"A two-step," Jackson Lord quipped.

Rick stared hard at him. "We can plan the quickness of other deaths."

"This," said Gloria, "is getting a little thick for me," She stood, looked momentarily at sea, then wandered toward the kitchen.

"I'm sorry," Jackson said to Rick, "but I think you're talking about murder."

Rick nodded. "Does it upset you?"

"Of course it upsets me. It would upset any caring person."

"Not the mere talk of it, Jackson," said Rick. He picked up his glass, looked down into it, said, "The mere talk of anything at all should upset no one."

"That's sophistic," said Professor Curtsinger.

"What's that?" said Maurice L'Oreal, who, if he had not been drunk, would never have admitted to an ignorance of the word "sophistic."

"Words explain our insides," said Curtsinger. "So they *are* our insides and they rule us."

"That there, I mean," Maurice said drunkenly. "On the rug. Is it a spider?" He pretended to sink back into his club chair.

"We dance in time," said Rick, who, though he hadn't touched alcohol in five years, could easily and convincingly mimic the mood of the drunken people he was sitting with—it was a way of keeping himself a part of the group, and sometimes he played the role so well he fooled even himself. "Time dances in us," he rephrased, and suddenly the group was off on another line of conversation.

The Following Morning

Ryerson, standing in Inspector Creed's office doorway, said, "I can help you, Dan."

"With what?"Creed grumbled.

"With the man in the cocoon," Ryerson answered. Creosote squirmed to be let down. Ryerson ignored him. "Dan, I want to help, I *need* to help."

"I'm sorry about what happened the other day, Rye, but at the moment I really don't know—"

"The man in the cocoon!" Ryerson cut in.

"Oh, shit!" Creed whispered.

"I can help you find the man who did it," Ryerson said.

"Why don't you sit down. I'll get us both some coffee—"

"He'll do it again," Ryerson cut in. "He's done it before, more than once. He can't help himself."

"Rye, I really don't know what in the hell you're talking about."

Creosote hopped out of Ryerson's arms and hit the floor face first. His front legs buckled, he flopped to his side, and for a moment looked as if he were dead. Then he pushed desperately at the air with his hind legs, righted himself, and scurried under the narrow opening at the front of Creed's desk.

"Oh, hell," Creed whispered, bent over, and looked under the desk. "Well come *here,* dog!"

"I'll get him," Ryerson said and went around to the front of Creed's desk, got down on all fours, and cooed, "It's okay, fella." Moments later, he scooped Creosote into his arms and stood.

A detective came in and put a file folder on Creed's desk. Creed opened the front of the file folder. An 8x10 of the body that had fallen through the false ceiling of the Commerce Court West Building lay beneath.

"That's him!" Ryerson shouted. "The man in the cocoon!"

EIGHT

I t's like having fourteen-hundred-foot-long legs,"
Harry Lamb—who was himself very tall and thin—
said.

His computer-matched date, short, chunky, round-
faced, pleasant-looking Loretta McPhee, standing with
him on the space deck—the highest observation level of
the 1,815-foot-tall CN Tower—murmured her assent,
then managed a quivering smile. It was a little past eight
in the evening. Below, the lights of Toronto twinkled like
tiny quartz chips on a gray sidewalk. Some 125 miles to
the south, the horizon was visible only as a change in the
texture of the darkness rather than in its color, from
matte to smooth.

The cement observation deck, which looked like a
huge tire placed horizontally on the tower 800 feet from
its tip, had windows around its interior so viewers could
look straight down the long, curving, lighted superstruc-
ture of the tower to the ground. Hence Harry's remark
about having 1,465-foot-tall legs.

"You're scared, aren't you?" he said now to Loretta
McPhee. "Don't be scared. This damned thing will be

here for another million years. It's sunk into the bedrock; it's a part of the earth itself. God, but that's impressive."

"Yes," Loretta managed, her voice slight and quivering, "I *am* scared, Harry. Can we go back down to the restaurant?" The revolving restaurant, and the disco—Sparkles, the Sky-High Nightclub—were on the 1,150-foot level.

"What for?" he asked.

"Dessert," she answered. Actually, it was the farthest thing from her mind. At this height, the idea of a hot fudge sundae, an apple turnover, or raspberry cheese-cake—her favorite—made her stomach feel as if it were on ball bearings and rolling crazily about.

"Sure," Harry said. "We can do dessert." He patted his flat belly beneath his green silk shirt. "The old food bin's about set for some more input."

Loretta burped.

"Ah," he said, putting his arm around her chunky shoulders, "but not yours, I think, my dear. I think this altitude is a little dizzying."

"I just don't have the faith that you have, Harry."

"What faith is that?"

"In other people. In the people who built this tower, I guess. You have to have unquestioning faith in them to comfortably stand up here. I just don't have it. I'm sorry. I *know* the tower's not going to fall—"

"But your heart's not convinced, eh?"

"Or my head. The deep insides of my head. Do you understand?"

"Yes." He smiled, amused. "Harry Lamb understands just about everything, my dear."

She burped again. "Thanks," she said. "Let's go back down now."

"Sure," he said. And they did.

Getting into Commerce Court West at this hour of the evening wasn't particularly difficult for Ryerson. The combination to the pushbutton-style lock that released the elevator was known to some 200 people, each of whom used the lock at least once or twice a week, when overtime demanded that they work late. So the set of five numbers was, almost literally, floating about in the air, like dust.

The guard was watchful, of course. If Ryerson spent too long at the lock, then, naturally, he had no business in the building. Getting past the guard himself had been a piece of cake. A woman named Barbara Ebert worked at the building and had left it recently. Her perfume still lingered in the air. The guard couldn't get her out of his mind. He also couldn't get out of his mind the fact that she had been married recently. The guard had never met her husband, but his jealousy bordered on rage. It was that rage—a rage he fought very hard to keep in check— that Ryerson played on.

"Can I help you, sir?" the guard had asked when Ryerson appeared.

"Yes." A pause; he probed about in the man's mind, sensed the lust and anger there. "Barbara left some papers here. She asked me to pick them up."

"And you are?"

"Her husband."

"Her husband?" Ryerson felt the man successfully

fight his rage down, and sublimate his caution with it. "Oh. Of course." And the guard had let him through to the elevators, where Ryerson encountered the combination locks. He looked back. The guard was watching. Ryerson tried to probe his mind for the combination. The man's anger blocked him. He breathed one of his rare curses, "Damn!" and set to work on the lock.

The numbers themselves came easily to him. They were 8, 9, 3, 0, 18. That was not, however, their correct order. That, he realized sinkingly, would be a matter of trial and error. He quickly pressed 0, then 9, 3, 8, and 18. Nothing. He tried 9, 3, 8, 0, 18. Still nothing. He knew this could take a long time. There were hundreds of possible sequences of those five numbers.

"Trouble?" he heard the guard call.

He glanced back. "No. No trouble." He paused. "Barbara gave me this combination—"

"She's not supposed to do that," the guard said, and Ryerson realized that the man's caution was finally winning out over his jealousy.

"Well, she did," Ryerson shrugged. "I'm sorry. But I forgot the sequence. Isn't it eight, nine, three—"

"Three's first," the guard called. "Then eight, nine, eighteen, and zero."

"Thanks," Ryerson called back, and pressed the numbers.

Minutes later, he was on the fifty-sixth floor.

Moving through the corridor where the body of Leonard Peters had fallen through the false ceiling was like moving through a stew. The air was thick not only with

Leonard himself—with his fears and regrets and memories (he had worked alone in the building for years)—but also with images of Leonard's killer. And that was the nasty spice of the stew. It stank, made Ryerson's eyes smart, clogged his senses. Images came and went as if on a swiftly revolving wheel—buildings, women, hair, naked backs, the smell of sweat and the smell of tar, shouted curses like huge, dung-colored flies. There was another image, too. One that seemed at once a part of all the others but somehow removed, as well, as if it were a part of the man, the murderer, and a part of something else, too—Ryerson had no idea what. It was the image of *people* shouldering closer to him, *people* hunched over and shouldering closer to him in the darkness. It was an awful, stifling image, and it was many minutes before Ryerson realized that he was not moving in the corridor, that the whole psychic stew boiling up here had stopped him cold.

Then, at once, the images ended. The wheel came to a halt, dissipated, and Ryerson found himself breathless, in shock. His psychic sense had overloaded and shut down.

He crumbled to a sitting position against the wall. He had never before experienced such an overwhelming flood of psychic input. It made him fearful—*Good Lord, such a creature as could leave behind that awful residue is loose in this city!* He shuddered and felt very cold.

Jason Granger, alone on the 1,465-foot level of the space-deck observation level of the CN Tower, his eyes on the rough blanket of darkness that stretched 125 miles in all directions, whispered, "This is very nice here." *It makes a person feel so . . . insignificant,* he thought, and wondered what appeal there was in being made to feel insignificant. He decided that it made his mistakes in life seem insignificant. In the great and grand scheme of things, it made him somehow blameless. It was nice to feel like that, especially after the way he had treated Laura and the kids. God but he'd have to do something about his temper. Lord knew what. What could he do about something like that? Something that was so controlling and, ironically, so out of control. Count to ten? That didn't work—he'd tried it. Professional help? Half of *those* guys were crazy as bedbugs themselves. And *there* was something. He wasn't *crazy* so much as . . . frustrated. He wasn't foaming at the mouth, wasn't running around on all fours and howling at the moon. He was *frustrated.* Life had dealt him a bad hand, and he had to play it.

So it was really nice being up here where none of that shit mattered, where it all amounted to far less, even, than one of those specks of light below. That was comforting. That made him feel good inside.

He closed his eyes. He sensed the sheer *bigness* of everything around him: the tower, the land below, the sky. The emptiness of this place.

He thought it would be nice to stay here forever.

He felt *people* around him, crowding close.

MID-MORNING, THE FOLLOWING DAY

"You know what it sounds like to me, Rye?" Dan Creed said into the phone. "It sounds like you're trying to redeem yourself."

"And is that so ignoble?" Ryerson asked.

"No. It's not ignoble. It's simply not necessary."

"Dan, I can help you."

Creed sighed. "We can use all the help we can get, Rye, but I'm afraid I can't get authorization for any further payments to you. Any help you give us will have to be in the nature of a gift."

"Of course," Ryerson said. "I'll be in touch."

Ryerson put the receiver on the hook, sighed, and turned to Creosote, gnawing at an argyle sock at the foot of the bed. "It looks like we've got to carry the ball alone on this one, fella."

Creosote gurgled.

Ryerson went to a window that overlooked downtown Toronto. Ten stories below, on the opposite side of Yonge Street, construction had just begun on "A Multilevel Shopping and Banking Facility," as the architect's sign proclaimed. Apparently, Ryerson thought, the word "skyscraper" had become passé.

Cement mixers were everywhere. A crane was lifting huge girders to the second-story level, where beefy construction workers guided them into place as if they were pieces in an Erector set. Ryerson had watched such work before, and it fascinated him. He knew that within a couple of days, the building's skeleton could be completed up to the seventh or eighth floor. Such speed was incredible. And dangerous. Men died as a result of it, because, as the cliché said, "Time is money." Put up a skyscraper in three-quarters the time allotted, and someone made a hell of a lot of money.

Ryerson thought that there was something unusual

about the men who worked the high steel. The fact that they displayed no fear as they walked on a girder at forty or fifty stories up was remarkable. But fear was destructive, Ryerson realized. It made people overly cautious and stiff. The men who worked high steel had to walk those girders in the same easy way that other people walked boardrooms or lines at the supermarket. But this attitude had to alter their sense of reality, Ryerson thought. Because a girder fifty stories up simply was not a line at the supermarket. If a man stepped the wrong way on line at the supermarket, he would simply have to go back to the end of the line. If a man stepped the wrong way on a girder fifty stories up, that man was history. Such men were therefore *alive* in a vital and consuming way that others simply weren't. And it was possible that, in the very act of falling from one of those girders, such men were more alive than they had ever been. It was a grisly idea.

Behind him, Creosote gurgled, wheezed, grunted, then leaped from the bed, ran over, and looked pleadingly up at him. Ryerson picked him up and stroked him at the back of the neck, which the dog loved. "Creosote," Ryerson whispered, "I think someone is still falling."

NINE

Ryerson didn't immediately recognize the chunky man in the ill-fitting white suit who was sitting in the lobby of the Sheraton Toronto. And because he didn't immediately recognize him, but knew he had seen him *somewhere,* his gaze lingered on him too long. Finally the man looked up from his Sunday edition of the *Toronto Sun Times,* a smile broke out on his round pink face, and he rose and ambled over, his hand extended.

"I've been waiting for you, Rye," the man said.

Ryerson sighed. It was Lenny Baker, the man who had wanted to play Watson to Ryerson's Sherlock Holmes.

"Nice dog, Rye," Baker added, nodding at Creosote, cradled in Ryerson's arms. Lenny still had his hand extended. Ryerson shook it quickly. "Good to see you, Mr. Baker," he said, and started for the revolving doors.

Lenny fell in beside him. He held the Sunday *Sun Times* out so Ryerson could see the front page. "Are you going to be looking into this, Rye?"

Ryerson glanced at the paper, saw the headline: BI-ZARRE MURDER AT COMMERCE COURT WEST. He stopped, took the paper from Lenny, and read the article quickly:

Police are looking for a suspect in the murder of Leonard Peters 54, a janitor employed at the Commerce Court West Building, on Bloor Street. Peters' body, wrapped in plastic, was found Tuesday. It had apparently fallen from above a false ceiling, where it had been tied to overhead pipes. According to the Medical Examiner's office, Peters had been dead at least two days before his body was found.

'It's a very strange case,' said Inspector Dan Creed of the Toronto Police Department's Homicide Division. 'Probably the strangest case I've ever dealt with. We're trying to find a parallel, which would help us locate a suspect, but so far our efforts have produced little of value.'

When asked if Ryerson H. Biergarten—the psychic detective called in to help in a recent missing-persons case—would help with this case, Creed replied, 'No. Mr. Biergarten will have no connection with our investigation.

Mr. Peters had been employed at the Commerce Court West for nine years—

Ryerson gave the newspaper back to Lenny. "No," he said. "I've been asked to stay clear, at least at an official level, and that's what I'm going to do."

Lenny was astonished. "Stay clear? By who? This guy Creed? Why? Did you louse up?"

Ryerson stared hard at him. "Yes, Mr. Baker. I loused up." He pushed through the revolving doors, turned left, and walked quickly toward Queen Street, heading for lunch at an outdoor café called The Coachman.

Lenny pushed through the revolving door and jogged heavily toward him. "Wait up!" he called. Moments later, he was puffing along beside Ryerson toward Queen Street. "Hey, Rye, you walk pretty fast."

"Yes, it's good for the heart."

"Not *my* heart."

Ryerson looked appraisingly at him. He stopped walking. Lenny stopped. Ryerson said, "What is it you want from me, Mr. Baker?"

"You can call me Lenny, Rye."

"Thank you."

Lenny pushed at his white suit coat to flatten it out—it had ridden up on his waist—then fished in his pants pocket, pulled out a crumpled pack of White Star Little Cigars, and held the pack up. "Cigar?"

"No," Ryerson answered. "I quit."

Lenny grinned apologetically, pulled one of the cigars from the pack, and stuck it in his mouth.

"So?" Ryerson coaxed.

"What do I want?"

"Yes."

"Just the chance to work with you. I've studied your career and your methods. I know everything there is to know about you, Rye. I know you've got an interest in this Commerce Court West thing, and I want to be a part of it."

"You're wrong, Lenny. I have no interest in it. I'm here on vacation—"

"I know you left for Boston two days ago, Rye."

This took Ryerson by surprise.

Lenny's grin reappeared. "See, Rye, I really am psychic, like I said."

"Many people are," Ryerson said and started walking again toward Queen Street.

Lenny kept pace. "I know you stopped somewhere south of the Canadian border. I don't know why you stopped, but I know that you did."

Ryerson kept walking. He looked at Lenny. "As I've told you, I work alone. I've always worked alone."

"Is that an admission that you're working on this Commerce Court West case?"

Ryerson stopped at the corner of Queen and Yonge to wait for the light. Around him, the curb edge began filling up with people also intent on going somewhere for lunch. Lenny whispered secretively, "Someone's going to scream, Rye."

Ryerson looked sideways at him.

Lenny explained, "In a few moments, before the light changes."

Someone screamed quickly, and shrilly. Ryerson turned his head sharply to the right. He saw a tall woman several feet away who wheeled around and slapped a man standing just behind her. "Pervert!" she cried. Then the light changed.

Ryerson looked at Lenny, then at the woman, who was halfway across the street and walking very stiffly, as if in anger, then at the man she'd slapped, who was rubbing his face, had his mouth open, and was shaking his head in confusion.

Lenny grinned from ear to ear. "I've got the gift, Rye."

"Of course you do," Ryerson said, then jogged across the street leaving Lenny at the curb.

* * *

Officer Stephen Lake poked his head into Inspector Creed's office. "Missing Persons is on the line for you, inspector."

"Missing Persons?"

Lake nodded. "Yeah. They say they've got something that might interest you."

Creed picked up the phone. "Inspector Creed here."

A woman at the other end said, "Sergeant Eady, Inspector. I've got a missing person report. Granger, Jason, age thirty-two, postal clerk—"

"This is homicide, Sergeant."

"Yes, Inspector, I know that. But this man—this Jason Granger—was last seen on the space-deck level of the CN Tower. I thought there could be a tie-in to this murder at the Commerce Court West Building."

Creed hesitated, then said, "Yes, okay. Go ahead."

"I'll send over our file on it, then."

"I'd appreciate it," Creed said.

An hour later, the file had been delivered, and Creed had gone over what little information was available on the Granger disappearance (the man's description, occupation, the names of people who had last seen him and where). He went immediately to the CN Tower's 1,465-foot Space Deck level—billed as "the highest observation deck in the world"—with Detective Max Tyler who, true to his habits, was shrugging a lot and pooh-poohing the whole idea of a link to the murder at Commerce Court West. "How could there be a connection, Dan?" he asked. "I mean, where's anyone going to hide a body up here?"

It was a good question. The Space Deck was simply a

circular glass-enclosed concrete observation deck, to which access was gained by an interior elevator that operated from the 1,165-foot "Skypod" observation level. The Space Deck had one storage closet, in a dark triangular area to the right of and behind the elevator, a solid black ceiling in which there were two one-foot-square electrical-wiring-access doors, two circular steel stairwells which led from the observation deck itself to the elevators, eight feet below. The steps were just over a foot wide, and solid; a landing several feet from the bottom of each stairwell was also solid metal and four feet square. A huge poster of the Matterhorn over the elevator—the doors to the elevator were dark red—was littered with graffiti and bumper stickers. One piece of graffiti read; "This elevator is good to the last drop." Creed was surprised at how seedy the place was.

Max Tyler had been up here a number of times, usually in an effort to impress various women with his nonchalance about being at such a dizzying height. His name was inscribed on a small rectangular copper plaque, as proof that he had been on the "highest observation deck in the world," and was therefore a member of the "Sky-High Club." The plaque was displayed, along with several thousand others, on the walls of a short hallway at the center of the Space Deck.

Creed had already interviewed the attendant on duty at the Space Deck elevator's Skypod entrance level; she had been on duty the night of Granger's disappearance:

"I remember him going up," she said. "He was alone. People don't usually go up there alone, you know. I mean, the *kick's* in being up there *with* someone, right? But he was alone. And he didn't come down."

"You're sure of that?"

She shook her head. "No. I'm not sure. He could have gotten past me when I wasn't looking. I mean, we tell everyone, 'Take the elevator down to the Skypod level; don't get out here.' But no one ever listens. They all get out here, and they run into people getting on, so they have to crawl under that railing." She nodded at a set of red-painted railings at right angles to her station; the railings led people to the ticket counter and then into the elevator, down a short, dark hallway.

"So, in other words, this man could have gotten out at the Skypod level—isn't that right?"

The ticket seller shrugged. "Sure. He could have. But Leslie was down there. She was on duty that night, and she says he never got past her."

"Oh," said Creed, and made a mental note to talk to Leslie.

The one closet, behind and to the right of the stairway, had been checked by a uniformed cop the morning after the disappearance. The same cop had even checked the electrical-wiring-access doors in the ceiling: "Jesus," he had said, "you couldn't hide a kitten up here, for God's sake!"

Tyler said now, "Like I told you before, Dan"—he shrugged—"this guy Granger is *somewhere's* else."

Except for Tyler and Creed, the Space Deck was empty. Four hundred feet below, the revolving restaurant was beginning to fill with business people. On the observation level, a family of five from Schenectady, New York was discussing the merits of riding the interior elevator to the Space Deck.

"*I'm* not going up there!" Paul, the husband, proclaimed. "If *you* want to get sick, Florence, then you're going to have to do it all by yourself." He had stayed well clear of the windows that overlooked Toronto 1,165 feet below, twice the height of the Washington Monument. In the exterior elevator that had brought him and his family to the Skypod level, he had kept his eyes closed tightly all the way and had swallowed hard several times to keep his ears from popping while the elevator operator droned on about the CN Tower's vital statistics.

Poking Paul playfully in the stomach with her forefinger, Florence said, "Chicken!"

"Yeah, daddy," chirped four-year-old Kevin. "Chicken!"

"Bawk, Bawk!" said Debby, who was eight.

Paul gave her a withering gaze. She shrank away from him and hid behind her mother. "Bawk, bawk!" she whispered.

"Besides," Paul began, but was upstaged by two-year-old Dorian, in Florence's arms, who let out with something that sounded like a cross between a war whoop and a belch. Paul grimaced. "I told you we shouldn't have had those clams last night," he said.

Florence announced, "Well *we're* going up! You can stay here if you like, Paul, but *we're* going up!" She marched over to where the red-painted steel rails curved tightly around to the ticket counter for the elevator ride to the Space Deck. The tickets were one dollar each,

Canadian. Florence looked back at her husband. "Paul, I need—" She looked at the ticket seller—the same woman who had talked to Dan Creed, the woman who had last seen Jason Granger.

Florence asked her, "Are the children free, miss?"

The woman nodded. "Under five, yes, ma'am."

Florence turned back to Paul, who was standing sullenly a couple of yards away. "Paul, I need three Canadian dollars."

Paul sighed, fished in his pocket a moment, pulled out a five, shuffled over, and handed it to her.

Seconds later, Florence and her three children went through the blood-red elevator doors and were on their way to the Space Deck observation level.

Where Dan Creed was saying, "Did anyone check the elevator?"

"The elevator?" Max Tyler said.

Creed nodded. "Up above it. Did anyone check there?"

Tyler shrugged.

Creed said, "You shrug too much. What is it, some kind of nervous twitch?"

Tyler shrugged again. "I guess so, Dan. I'm sorry."

"Don't be. As long as you're aware of it."

"Sure, Dan. And no, I don't think anyone checked above the elevator."

Creed shrugged. "Maybe we should."

"Maybe," Tyler said. They started down one of the sets of circular black steel stairwells which led to the elevator level eight feet below.

That's when two of Florence's children—four-year-old Kevin, and eight-year-old Debby—erupted from the elevator and clambered up the opposite stairwell while Florence, who was having second thoughts about being up here, began to shift two-year-old Dorian from one arm to the other. "You're getting heavy, little man!" she cooed, though her voice had a quiver of nervousness in it.

Dorian dropped his plastic bottle of orange juice then, while he was being shifted from one arm to the other. The bottle was nearly empty, so when it hit the concrete floor, it rolled. "Damn!" Florence breathed, stooped over, and began to pad after it. The bottle hit the wall near the circular stairwell. Florence put Dorian on the floor. He stood quietly for a moment, confused that the building he was in seemed to be swaying slightly, then toddled toward the stairwell.

Behind Florence, Tyler and Creed had reached the elevator level and were pressing the button for service. There was no "DOWN" or "UP" button. Everything was down from here.

Dorian pointed under the four-foot-square solid-steel landing which was just a few feet away from where his mother was retrieving his nearly empty bottle.

Tyler said, "I've been up here before, you know. I like it up here."

"Good for you," Creed said.

"I'm not afraid of heights. I was going to work in construction once. On the high steel—that's what they call it, Dan. The 'high steel.' "

"I know that's what they call it," Creed said. He added, clearly miffed, "You know, that would be the first place I'd check if I were looking for a body up here. I'd look over the elevator."

Two-year-old Dorian was still pointing to the area under the black solid-steel landing, "Look!" he said. "Bag in there!"

TEN

The following afternoon, Ryerson Biergarten, having a lunch of *gnocchi piemontese* and green salad at the Gran Festa Ristorante on Front Street West, only blocks from the CN Tower, found the front page of the *Toronto Star* shoved under his nose. He stared at it a few moments, then let his gaze rise very slowly and deliberately up the arm of the person holding the newspaper, then to the person's face. It was Lenny Baker, and he was grinning.

Ryerson said, "Hello, Mr. Baker."

Lenny nodded at the newspaper. "Go ahead. Read it."

"I'm having lunch, Mr. Baker." Actually, the gnocchi had yet to arrive; Ryerson was nursing a cup of espresso—the Gran Festa did not serve regular coffee.

Lenny's chubby pink grin faded. He went around, sat leadenly in the chair opposite Ryerson, and held the newspaper up so Ryerson could read a bold headline halfway down the page. The headline read: BODY FOUND IN CN TOWER

Lenny asked, "Did you know about this, Rye?"

"I knew about it."

Lenny shook his head. "No, I mean *before* you read it in the paper. *I* did."

"You did what?"

"I knew about it before I read it in the paper."

"I'm happy for you," Ryerson said.

The waiter came over. "Yes, sir?" he said to Lenny.

Ryerson looked up at the waiter. "This gentleman is joining me, I imagine."

Lenny asked, "What kind of spaghetti you got?"

"Here's a menu, sir," the waiter answered, smiling, and gave Lenny a menu.

Lenny looked it over. "What's this *'vitello tonnato'*?" he asked, then hurried on, "No, wait. Why don't you bring me a ham-and-cheese sandwich. Heavy on the mayo. And put it on rye bread."

"Yes, sir," the waiter said to Lenny. He took the menu back and added, "Anything to drink, sir?"

"You got root beer?" Lenny asked.

"No, sir. Coca-Cola."

"No Pepsi?"

"No, sir. Just Coke."

"Pepsi's better. You should get some Pepsi."

Ryerson stood. The waiter looked up at him. "Sir?"

"I'm leaving," Ryerson told him.

"But your gnocchi, sir."

Ryerson nodded at Lenny Baker. "He can have it."

Lenny frowned like a sad pink pumpkin. "Don't leave, Rye," he said. "I'm sorry."

The waiter said to Lenny, "Sir, would you prefer the gnocchi or the ham-and-cheese on rye?"

"Sorry for what?" Ryerson asked Lenny.

"For tricking you the other day."

"Then you admit it?"

"Yes."

The waiter asked Lenny. "Gnocchi and Coca-Cola, then?"

"Yes."

"It was you in that car, wasn't it?" Ryerson asked.

"What car?"

"It will be only a moment, sir," said the waiter. "Sir," he added, turning his attention to Ryerson, "are you still going to be dining with us?"

Ryerson sighed. "Sure. Why not?"

"Oh," Lenny said, "you mean the one that hit the deer, don't you?"

"Yes," Ryerson answered. "And that's how you knew I turned around and came back to Toronto, isn't it?"

"Gnocchi for both of you?" the waiter said. "Fine. And Coca-Cola. I'll bring you more espresso, sir."

"Yes," Lenny said to Ryerson. "And you're right. I *did* set up that thing on the street."

"Oh, for heaven's sake, Lenny. I knew that the moment it happened. You forget—"

"Who you are, Rye? No, I don't. But when I tell you that *I'm* psychic, too—"

"Yes. I know you are." Ryerson sighed. "But let me reiterate: I work alone. I really don't need your help."

Lenny grinned. "We'll see."

In an Office Building on Yonge Street, Near Bloor Street West

The red-haired woman stuck her head in through the open doorway. "Rick?"

Rick looked up from the newspaper on his desk. "Yes, Roberta?"

"Three o'clock appointment, Rick. You've got ten minutes. I'm sorry I didn't remind you sooner—"

"Oh, hell!" Rick said peevishly. He ran his hand through his full head of graying dark brown hair. "Who's it with?" he sighed.

"The people from the Ministry of Parks and Recreation," Roberta answered. "You remember, they've wanted to see your final plans for the pavilion at the Science Center—"

"I can never get over that," Rick cut in. He stood and brushed at his gray suit pants to smooth them out. " 'The Ministry' of this, and 'the Ministry' of that." He smiled. Roberta, who was a native Canadian and very patriotic, forced herself to smile back. Rick went on, "It's all so . . . stuffy and Victorian. Know what I mean?"

Roberta's smile flattened. "I rather like it, Rick."

Rick nodded. "Yes, of course you do. You're Canadian, after all. But you can understand how it sounds to a guy from the east side of Chicago, right?"

"I think so." She checked her watch. "Eight minutes now. I've called for a taxi. It should be waiting for you downstairs."

Rick sighed again. He came around from behind his desk slowly, as if in thought, stopped midway to the door, and shoved his big hands into his pants pockets. "There's no way I can get out of it, is there?"

Roberta shook her head. "Not this time, Rick."

"I'd really like to. Tell them the plans aren't ready, why don't you. Tell them I've made some revisions. Tell them there was an error in the load-bearing calculations—"

Roberta looked at her wristwatch. "Five minutes now, Rick." She turned and went back to her desk.

"Shit!" Rick breathed.

"He shoved him under the landing!" Lenny Baker exclaimed, smiling and holding up the front page of the *Toronto Star*. He pointed to the article headlined BODY FOUND IN CN TOWER and added, "The maniac wrapped this guy up in plastic and shoved him under the landing." His smile grew crooked. "Isn't that a hoot!"

Ryerson took a bite of his *gnocchi piemontese.*

"Hey," Lenny observed, "you didn't get your salad, where's your salad?"

"It comes second," Rye answered. "It's better for the digestion that way."

"Oh," Lenny said. "Yeah, sure." He turned the *Toronto Star* around and started reading it aloud, and loudly, as if he were giving a shrill speech to anyone within earshot:

"According to Detective Inspector Dan Creed, the plastic in which the body was wrapped had started to swell due to the escape of gases from—"

"Shutup!" Ryerson whispered tightly.

"Huh?" Lenny said.

"Good Lord, man, this is a *restaurant*!"

Lenny shook his head. "No, Rye—it's a 'Ristorante.' " He grinned at his little joke.

Ryerson sighed. "I've read the article. I know about the swelling plastic, I know the name of the victim, I know what the police have said about the murder. So, please, please, let's not discuss it right now."

"I know more," Lenny announced, and folded the newspaper up and put it in the inside pocket of his wrinkled, cream-colored, cotton suit jacket.

Ryerson looked silently at him with a forkful of gnocchi halfway to his mouth.

Lenny repeated, "I know more," paused and added, "I know this guy's a dancer."

Ryerson popped the forkful of gnocchi into his mouth.

"I'm not talking about the victim, this Jason Granger," Lenny clarified. "I'm talking about the murderer."

Ryerson sipped his espresso.

"It came to me in a dream, Rye," Lenny continued.

Ryerson smiled noncommittally.

"Last night," Lenny said. "Early this morning, really. That's when I dream. I think it's when most people dream, don't you? And I saw him there—this guy, in my dream, and he was dancing, kind of—I mean, he wasn't mincing around, he was dancing, you know, and I knew that he was this murderer. I knew he was this maniac who wraps people up in plastic. I didn't see his face. It was like he had a stocking over it; it was hazy and I couldn't see his features, so I can't tell you if he was good looking or ugly or whatever—"

"He's not a dancer," Ryerson interrupted.

"Huh?" Lenny said.

"The image you got . . . the *dream* you had was only partial, it was only a small part of the picture."

Lenny got his ham-and-cheese on rye. He started on it at once. Through a mouthful of shredded lettuce and bread, he said, "You're telling me I'm wrong?"

Ryerson shook his head. "Not wrong, only partly correct."

Lenny swiped at his mouth with the back of his hand. "What do you know that I don't?"

"Only that he's not a dancer. That he feels he has power. Sometimes. That perhaps the man who's doing these murders is not the man who's responsible for them."

Lenny stopped his mouth in mid-chew. "Huh?"

"Possessed," Ryerson said. "Our murderer is a man possessed. I'm absolutely positive of it."

ELEVEN

M ax Tyler looked across his desk at Dan Creed, who was brushing the sugar from a sugar doughnut into his wastebasket. "Dan?" Tyler said.

Creed looked up. "Yes?"

"There's a woman named McPhee on the phone. She says she's got information on the Granger homicide."

"Another loony, you think?"

Tyler shook his head. "I don't think so. Do you want to talk to her?"

Creed nodded and picked up his phone. "Yes, this is Detective Inspector Creed. What can I do for you?"

Loretta McPhee said, with a high nervous squeak at the end of her sentences, "My name is Loretta McPhee. I live in Toronto—in Yorkville, really. And I was at the tower, the CN Tower, on the night this man was killed."

"Go on."

"Yes, certainly." She paused. "I was with a man, a stranger. Not really a stranger, of course. I don't go out with strangers."

"Certainly."

"His name is Harry Lamb, and he lives in Toronto.

Downtown somewhere. I'm not sure where. West of Yonge Street. Near Bloor Street, I think. He lives in a hotel near Bloor Street."

"And?"

"And he was my date for the night. Only for the night. We were . . . computer matched through Datago, and he was my date."

"Miss McPhee, perhaps you could tell me the reason for your call."

"Well, I've told you that, haven't I? I was in the CN Tower with this man, Harry Lamb, on the night that the murder happened, and I think he did it."

"Why do you think that, Miss McPhee?"

She didn't answer.

"Miss McPhee?"

"I don't know, for sure." She hesitated. "Just a feeling. He was very strange—well, not *very* strange, really. I don't go out with *very* strange men. Actually, you don't know who's going to be just plain strange, and who's going to be *very* strange until you *do* go out with them, do you? But maybe that's not so. I mean, *very* strange people are usually locked up somewhere, aren't they? *Very* strange people don't do videotapes for Datago—"

"Miss McPhee, perhaps if you could stick to the subject . . ."

"You're right. I'm sorry. I'm nervous. I've never gone out with a murderer before."

"That has not been established, Miss McPhee."

"Well, I haven't."

Creed sighed. "Could you give me your address and phone number, Miss McPhee, and could you tell me again where you think this man you went out with lives?"

"Yes," she said, and did.

It was raining heavily when Ryerson left the Gran Festa Ristorante, walked four blocks east to the CN Tower, then went up to the tower's 1,465-foot Space Deck level. Lenny Baker went up with him. Ryerson didn't want to go up in the tower with Lenny. He wanted to go up alone because, as he had already told Lenny, that's the way he worked. Alone.

But the sidewalk, Lenny pointed out, was a public place (and he began to walk several feet behind Ryerson, under his own umbrella, so Ryerson got soaked), and so, too, he proclaimed, was the CN Tower. Lenny took the number-two elevator up to the Skypod level, while Ryerson took elevator number one, although they went through the blood-red doors of the Space Deck elevator together, followed by an old couple who were wearing sheepish grins.

"I don't know, Mother," said the old man, who was dressed in a baggy gray suit. "I'm not sure I like this."

"Oh, of course you do, you old poop," said the woman. "They took the poor man away already. It's not as if we're going to *see* him. And so what if we did? Would it be any different from seeing one of the calves being slaughtered so people can have veal cutlets with their spaghetti? No, of course it wouldn't."

"Well, you're right of course, Mother. You're always right."

Lenny was smiling to himself, Ryerson noticed.

"And you should know better than to suggest that that

alone is the reason we are going up here. It is, after all, the tallest building in the world—"

"It's not a building, Mother. It's a freestanding structure."

"Not a building? If it's not a building, then what in the Sam hell is it—a blowfish?"

Lenny hooted.

"And you"—the old woman scolded—"mind your own damn business!"

"Yes, ma'am," Lenny said, forcing down a grin.

The elevator got to the Space Deck level. The doors opened. Lenny let the old couple out first, then he got out, followed by Ryerson.

"Where's your little dog, Rye?" Lenny asked.

"In my hotel room," Ryerson answered. "Sick, nursing a cold."

Lenny guffawed. "How could you tell, Rye—he does so much snorting and belching and growling, anyway."

But Ryerson wasn't listening. He was a couple of feet in front of the elevators; the old couple was going up one of the sets of metal stairs that led to the observation level—"Which landing do you think it was, Mother?" . . . "How, how in the Sam hell would I know? *That* one, probably. See the chalk?"—and he was dead still. His breathing was very shallow. His arms were stiff at his sides, his head erect, his eyes wide open and unblinking.

"Rye?" Lenny said. "Hey, you okay, buddy?"

Ryerson didn't answer.

"Well, would you look at him!" said the old woman, who had gotten to the top of the metal stairway and had turned her head to look at the opposite landing.

Seeing Ryerson, the old man said to Lenny, "Is your friend okay?"

Lenny grinned dumbly. "Yeah. Sure. I guess he does this now and again, you know. Kind of like a fit, maybe." He put a hand on Ryerson's shoulder. "Hey, c'mon, buddy, snap out of it!"

Ryerson's lips moved slightly.

The old man at the top of the stairway said, "I think you should call a doctor, young fella. There's a phone up here somewhere."

"And *I* think we should mind our own business, Freddy," said his wife.

"In the name of heaven, Mother, the man's in trouble."

Lenny was growing nervous. "No, no, it's okay. Really. He gets this way sometimes."

Ryerson groaned softly.

The old woman's mouth fell open. "Is he going to vomit?"

Lenny's grin grew broader. "No, I don't think so. I think he's going to talk." He turned to Ryerson. "Isn't that right, pal?"

"I . . ." Ryerson moaned.

The old man at the top of the stairs started back down. His wife called after him, "And where in the Sam hell do you think *you're* going, Freddy?"

"To help this man, if I can," Freddy answered.

"I can dance," Ryerson moaned. He tilted his angular, handsome head toward Lenny. "I can dance," he repeated.

"Sure you can, Rye. I bet you're a great dancer."

"I have power. I can dance." He grinned a strange, lopsided grin.

The old woman at the top of the stairs said, "That man's positively spooky." She paused. "Freddy, you come back here!"

Freddy stopped halfway down the stairs. "Uh, yeah," he said, betraying his heavy Maine accent.

"Come back here!" the old woman bellowed.

"I have power. I can dance," Ryerson repeated, and took a slow, lurching step forward.

The old man backed quickly, if clumsily, up the stairs.

"Now, Freddy!" screeched the old woman.

"What are you doin', Rye?" Lenny asked. "You're scaring me!"

Ryerson took another step forward, not quite so slow and lurching as his first.

The old man on the stairway was only a few steps from his wife, now.

Lenny said, "Rye, I don't like this."

"I have power," Ryerson crooned. "I can dance."

And with exquisite grace, he ran up the stairway, past the old man, whose mouth was hanging open, and whose eyes were wide with fear, past the old woman—who swung futilely at him with her purse, and squawked, "Don't you dare, don't you dare!"—and out onto the observation deck.

Lenny waddled up the stairs after him.

At this level, the observation deck was fully enclosed. There was a cement wall to waist level, and an outward-jutting V of thick, unbreakable glass beyond it. Ryerson, the earth 1,465 feet below, was standing on that V of glass when Lenny found him. He had his hands and face pressed hard into it. He was weeping.

And Lenny, watching him, felt *crowded*. He felt as if there were people pushing him on all sides.

Dan Creed had his shield out when Harry Lamb answered his door at the Brownstone Hotel. "Police. I'm Detective Inspector Creed. This is Detective Max Tyler. Your name is Harry Lamb?"

Lamb tilted his head in confusion. "Is something wrong? Is this about those parking tickets from last year? I'm going to pay them. All I need is a little time."

"No, sir," Creed said, and pocketed his shield. "It's not about parking tickets. You are Harry Lamb?" he repeated.

"Yeah, that's me. If it's not about parking tickets, then what's it about?"

"Could we talk to you inside, Mr. Lamb?"

"About *what*?" Harry insisted.

"About murder," Max Tyler said.

Harry's mouth fell open. "Murder? Whose murder? I didn't murder anyone!"

"We'd simply like to talk to you about anything you may have seen in the CN Tower three nights ago," Creed told him.

Harry smiled coyly. "It was her, wasn't it? Loretta McPhee? Tight-assed bitch!"

"May we come in and talk to you, Mr. Lamb?" Creed interrupted. "Or shall we have a talk downtown?"

"You know what you guys remind me of? That old TV series, the one with Jack Webb. *Dragnet.* But, let me tell you something—I know my rights, and I know I don't have to talk to you unless you get a warrant."

"No, Mr. Lamb," Creed said. "We don't have a warrant. We don't need one simply to talk to you. Now, either we come into your room, or you come downtown. Which is it going to be?"

Harry slammed his door.

Creed reacted instantly. He kicked the door hard below the knob and burst into the room with his .38 police special drawn and ready.

Max followed him, his .38 also drawn.

Lamb threw up his hands. Behind him, on the table beneath an open window, a whitish substance wafted into the air in a gentle breeze. Harry grinned nervously. "It's okay, guys. Just a little coke, that's all. Just a little nose candy."

Creed snapped, "On the floor. Spread 'em!"

Harry fell to the floor, facedown, and spread his legs and arms. He continued to protest, "Hey, guys, it's just a little coke. Where's the harm?"

Creed ordered, "Close the window, Max, and get that stuff secured."

Max went to the window, closed it, and scooped what remained of the cocaine into a Baggie on the table.

Creed leaned over Harry Lamb and patted him down for weapons.

"Clean?" Max asked.

"Yeah," Creed answered.

Harry Lamb protested, "Just because I do coke doesn't mean I go around cutting people up."

"That," said Creed, "is something we'll have to find out for ourselves."

TWELVE

A jowly middle-aged man in a stiff gray suit—one of a half-dozen people seated at a big circular oak table on the fiftieth floor of an office building on Bloor Street West—said to Rick, who was seated opposite them all, as if before a panel of judges, "I'm sorry, sir, but the plans you submitted to this committee are not acceptable. Our engineers found problems in a number of areas—most importantly in the stress calculations applicable not only to the subbasement load points, but also—"

Rick held up his hand. "Listen," he said, and leaned over the table and smiled wearily, "I know there are problems with this design. I tried to tell you people that, didn't I? I wanted more time with it. I wanted to sit down with your engineers and review—"

The jowly man cut in. "I'm sorry, sir, but we have given you every opportunity to avail yourself of our engineers, and you have not done so."

"You have?" Rick was confused. "Really? When?"

A thin, square-faced woman explained, "A number of times, sir. I have here, in fact, a half-dozen letters which this firm sent to you inviting you to avail yourself of the expertise of our engineers. But you never responded. And you never met with our engineers. Sir, we gave you this contract not only because we believed in your work, but also as a gesture of our goodwill as Canadians—"

"Shit!" spat Rick. " 'Goodwill as Canadians,' my ass!"

"Sir, please," the jowly man sputtered.

Rick pushed on, "Your so-called 'Canadian goodwill' is a lot of horse manure, my friend. *I* was the best man for the job, and you knew it. Otherwise you'd have hired someone else. Don't try to con me."

"Yes," said the woman. "You're right. Our goodwill had very little to do with our decision to hire you. However, sir, what you *once* were is not reflected in the designs you gave us. I've seen better work from first-year architecture students, and I believe I speak for all of us when I say that not only are we releasing you from this contract, but you're damned good and lucky we aren't suing you for the return of money already paid."

Rick stared at her a moment. Then he stood up, gathered some papers on the table together, put them in his briefcase, and left the room.

"Why were you up in the tower, Harry?" Creed asked. They had brought Harry Lamb into the station house, and he was seated in a straight-backed metal chair in the interrogation room.

Lamb sighed and shook his head. "This is getting to be a bore, guys. I mean, why's anyone go up in the tower? To see the fucking sights, right? To take some chickie up there and impress the hell out of her and see the fucking sights."

Creed said, "But you didn't impress her, did you, Harry?"

"So boil me in chicken fat. I didn't score. So what?"

"And that got you mad, didn't it?"

Harry sighed again. "What it got me was lover's nuts—"

"It got you so mad, in fact," Creed insisted, "that you came back later and waited for Jason Granger to show up—"

"Oh, hell, if I really did go back up there, wouldn't someone have seen me?"

"You know the answer to that question as well as we do, Harry. You're throwing up a smoke screen. Why?"

Harry sighed. "I want my lawyer."

"Harry, talk to us."

"The only thing I'm going to say to you is what my lawyer tells me to say."

"That's not smart, Harry."

"There you go sounding like Joe Friday again."

"Just tell us why you did it."

"I didn't."

"Tell us why you did it and, believe me, you'll feel a lot better."

"Did you rehearse that?"

"C'mon, Harry. Get it off your chest. You went up there, you tried to score, you didn't, you got mad—"

"What are you saying? That every guy who doesn't score goes out and kills someone?"

"No. Not everyone."

"Just me, huh? The coke-head."

"Talk to us."

"Go to hell!"

"Every journey begins with the first step."

"Let me write that down and put it in my wallet."

"You talk to us and life will be much, much easier for you."

"Goddammit, I told you, the only one I'm going to talk to is my lawyer."

And so it went.

At Queen's Hospital, five miles north of Toronto, the doctor in charge at the Psychological Evaluation and Testing Center asked Ryerson, "So you believe you're psychic, Mr. Biergarten?"

"Yes." Ryerson was seated on a steel examination table with his hands clasped over his knees and his head lowered. He was wearing a white hospital gown.

"And that is why," the doctor continued, "you were doing what you were doing in the CN Tower?"

"Yes."

"How long have you had these . . . impulses, Mr. Biergarten?" The doctor was a tall, thin, balding, no-nonsense man in his early fifties.

"I don't have impulses," Ryerson answered, his voice a low monotone. "I have reactions." His head was still lowered. He was fighting off the effects of a tranquilizer.

"Can you look up at me?" the doctor said.

Ryerson raised his head. The doctor looked first in

Ryerson's right eye, then his left. "Thank you. You can lower your head." Ryerson did it. The doctor continued, "Were you trying to jump from the tower?"

"No."

"Then what were you doing?"

"I was trying to fly."

"Is there a difference?"

"Yes."

"And that difference is?"

"Sorry?"

"And that difference is?"

"What difference?"

"The difference between jumping and flying."

"Do you know that your lover has a yeast infection?"

The doctor said nothing.

Ryerson continued, "She gets them quite often." His head was still lowered; he was still speaking in a low, weary monotone. "She gets them once every few months. The problem is very deeply rooted. The problem is with you, doctor."

The doctor managed, "We're straying." He glanced furtively about the room, as if someone were listening.

"Yes," Ryerson said. "We're straying."

"Let's not . . . do that," said the doctor. He smiled his flattest, most professional smile. "Let's stick to the topic at hand."

"By what right are you keeping me here?" Ryerson asked. He raised his head. The tranquilizer was wearing off.

The doctor answered, still smiling flatly, "The Mental

Hygiene Law of 1938 provides for temporary involuntary incarceration of any individual who demonstrates that he is a danger either to himself or to others."

"Oh," said Ryerson, and lowered his head once again.

"And that, I'm afraid, is you, Mr. Biergarten."

"Your wife doesn't know about your lover, does she, doctor?"

The doctor said nothing.

"And it would probably be of little consequence to her if your lover were not as young as she is."

The doctor whispered, "This is incredible."

Ryerson looked up. "I'm sorry, doctor, but I can't fool around here answering your questions. I have work to do."

The doctor shook his head quickly, in clear frustration. "But I . . . have no lover, Mr. Biergarten," he stammered.

Ryerson managed a weary smile. "I'm not making a value judgment, doctor. I can see that this . . . woman brings you happiness."

"Yes . . . yes," whispered the doctor.

"But if you want it in a word," Ryerson said, "then the word is blackmail. Either I get out of here immediately—"

The doctor shook his head again. "That's not necessary, Mr. Biergarten. Yes. I believe you. I'll sign the papers."

Ryerson nodded. "The happiness she brings you, Doctor, is a very good thing. I can see that."

"Thank you," the doctor said.

"I assume someone will bring me my clothes?"

"Immediately."

Lenny Baker was sitting on a blue vinyl couch in the hospital lobby. He'd been waiting for Ryerson, and as Ryerson approached, heading for the front doors, Lenny stood, smiled his huge, pink, aging cherub kind of smile and extended his chunky hand. Ryerson stared at it a moment, then shook it quickly. "Thank you," he said, and started for the doors.

Lenny looked crestfallen after him. "That's all?" he called. "God, Rye, I practically saved your life—"

Ryerson stopped and looked back. "I wasn't going to jump. I couldn't have, even if I'd wanted to."

"Sure," Lenny said, and went over to him. "I know that. But you could have fallen through accidentally. And if it weren't for me, you probably would have."

Ryerson was stymied. He shrugged. "Okay, then again, my thanks. I mean it, Mr. Baker. Thank you very much." He sighed. "Listen, do you want the truth?"

"Sure. Of course. Doesn't everyone?"

"No. But this is the truth between you and me: I don't like your methods, Mr. Baker. That's not a value judgment, and it's not something personal. I don't dislike *you* as a person. Actually, you're kind of endearing, in a bumbling way. But professionally, I'd say we're simply not compatible,"

Lenny grinned toothily. "I'll change my methods, then."

"I doubt very much that you can."

"You think I'm fat and disgusting, don't you? You can't deny it—I'm just as psychic as you are. I can read it in you—"

"I don't think you're fat and disgusting."

"I jog, you know. I just started. I do one mile every morning. Next week it'll be two miles, and the week after that it'll be three miles—"

"I told you—I do not find you fat and disgusting. That's not the issue; it's not the problem." Again he started for the doors. He felt Lenny's hand on his shoulder. He stopped, looked back.

Lenny said, with a Cheshire-cat smile, "The police got somebody for that CN Tower murder, Rye."

Ryerson said nothing.

Lenny added, "I heard it over the TV in there." He nodded toward a small room to the left of the lobby.

"Who?" Ryerson said. "Did you get a name?"

Lenny nodded. "Yeah. Some guy named Lamb."

"This is incredible," Ryerson said. "They've got the wrong man." He wasn't speaking to Lenny, he was speaking to himself. "That's all there is to it. The idiots have got the *wrong damned man.*"

"Yeah," said Lenny, "I know it, you know it, the guy they got knows it, but that's all that knows it."

Ryerson continued shaking his head. He turned quickly and headed for the front doors. Lenny fell in behind him. On the street, Ryerson hailed a cab, got in, saw Lenny getting in with him, said, "No. Please, no!" And there was such desperate urgency in his voice that Lenny backed away and hailed his own cab.

"Follow that car!" Lenny said to the driver.

"What car?" asked the driver.

"That one!" Lenny yelled, pointing stiffly at Ryerson's cab.

"Why?" asked the driver.

"What do you mean, 'Why?' I want you to follow it, that's all."

The driver turned around, smiling. "Listen, this is not some scene out of a Doris Day comedy. I am not going to follow that cab—it's not my business to follow cabs. It's my business to take people places and to obey all traffic regulations at the same time. If I have to successfully follow that cab, it will doubtless mean breaking several of those regulations, with the possible revocation of my license to drive. Therefore, as much as I'd like to comply with your wishes to, as you put it, 'Follow that cab!' I'm afraid that I can't. And I won't. If you wish to 'follow that cab,' you will have to do it on foot, or perhaps rent a bicycle."

"Shit!" Lenny breathed and hopped out.

The driver leaned over and said out the passenger window, "However, if you have knowledge of that cab's destination, well, that would be a different matter entirely. I could simply take you there, and you could . . ."

"Twelfth Precinct!" Lenny snapped and hopped back in.

Ryerson said to Creed, "You're holding someone for the CN Tower murder, aren't you, Dan?"

"Yes, we are," Creed answered. "Are you going to tell me we've got the wrong man?"

Ryerson nodded. "Actually, you do."

Detective Creed grinned. "Well, I'm one up on you. I know we've got the wrong man."

Ryerson was surprised. "And yet you're continuing to hold him?"

"On another charge, yes. But for now, it's probably best politically to let the public believe that we've got a suspect. It might also make the real murderer . . . careless."

"I've gotten images of the real murderer, Dan," Ryerson broke in.

Creed sighed.

"It's someone who lives in Toronto," Ryerson said.

"Tell me why that's not the astounding revelation of the month, Rye."

Ryerson added, "It's someone in power, someone who has authority."

Creed said, "Someone in authority, Rye? What's that supposed to be, a joke? 'Someone in authority' is a description of anyone over twenty-one with an IQ larger than my hat size."

Ryerson shook his head. "I'm trying to make sense of it, myself. It's a man in authority, a man who has power—"

"A man who has power over *what,* Rye?"

"I'm not sure. I don't know." A smile of recognition came to him. "Yes," he said. "I *do* know. It's a man who has power over . . . buildings." He paused. "Buildings," he repeated.

Creed laughed. "What's that mean, Rye? Our killer is a *janitor*?"

Ryerson looked confused. "A janitor? No, I don't think so, Dan. I don't think so. I think it's an architect." He hesitated very briefly. "Dan, I *know* it's an architect."

Creed let a little smile play on his lips. He opened one of his desk drawers, pulled out the Toronto yellow pages—a book two inches thick—and opened to the section listed *Architects.* He flipped one page. Then another. And another. He looked up at Ryerson. His smile faded. He said, "At a guess, I'd say there are three hundred architects listed here." He flipped back to the beginning of the section and pointed at what Ryerson knew was the first listing. "Shall we go talk to 'Aadman, Carl,' first?" Then"—he lowered his finger slightly—" 'Aldeman, Judy,' then 'Arlington, Graham,' then—"

Ryerson cut in, "It's a man. I know that."

Creed nodded. "Wonderful. That lowers the field to maybe two hundred seventy-five possible suspects. And tell me this, Rye—even if you were able to give me a name, what am I supposed to do with it? You give me a name—you give me 'Joe Schmo'—and what am I supposed to do? Am I supposed to go to a judge and say, 'Judge, this psychic says that Joe Schmo is our tower killer. Give me a warrant, okay?' If that sounds stupid, Rye, it's because it is."

"If I gave you a name, Dan, you'd know who to watch. I don't have to tell you that."

Creed regarded Ryerson for several moments. Then he said, "You're still trying to make amends, aren't you?"

"Amends for what?" Ryerson asked angrily.

"You know very well for what. For screwing up the

Cobb disappearance. That was a real blow to your pride, wasn't it, Rye? That hit you where you live."

Ryerson sighed. "Yes. I'll admit it. But what motivates me, or *appears* to motivate me shouldn't be of any concern to you, Dan. As long as I can help."

Creed turned his attention suddenly to the doorway. "What the hell are you doing here?"

Before Ryerson turned to look, he knew who Creed was talking to. He heard Lenny Baker say, "Hi, Dan. Me and Ryerson Biergarten here are working together. You didn't know that, did you?"

Ryerson shook his head slowly, in exasperation. "No, we aren't," he whispered.

Creed didn't hear him. "I thought you had better judgment, Rye. This guy's the biggest con man in Toronto."

"*Used* to be the biggest con man in Toronto, Dan," Lenny corrected. "I've gone straight."

Ryerson turned his head. "Do you have any idea of the trouble you're causing me, Mr. Baker?"

And, while Lenny was thinking of something to say, Ryerson said, to no one in particular, "His name is Rick."

THIRTEEN

*F*renzy was a good word. It fit. Like being on a merry-go-round. Like being in a blender. Like being in a cement mixer.

A cement mixer?

Rick pressed his intercom button. "Roberta, do I have any appointments this afternoon?"

"No," came her voice over the intercom. "You had one with the Toronto Architectural Board, but you canceled it."

"I did?"

"Yes, sir."

"Do you know why?"

"You canceled it because you were ill."

"When was that?"

"Yesterday."

"I wasn't ill yesterday."

"No, sir. You asked me to tell them you had a forty-eight-hour flu. That's the phrase you used—'a forty-eight-hour flu.' I've rescheduled the appointment for the twenty-ninth." A pause. "Is that all, sir?" She got no response. "Mr. Dunn?" Still nothing. "Are you okay, sir?"

"No," he answered, his voice suddenly low and hoarse. "I'm confused."

After several seconds of silence, Roberta said, "Confused about what, Mr. Dunn?"

"I need to see a priest, Roberta."

She said nothing.

Rick Dunn went on, his voice still very low and hoarse, "A Roman Catholic priest. Can you get one for me?" There was a hard urgency in his voice, as if he were pleading for air.

Roberta said, "I'll look in the yellow pages, Mr. Dunn."

Rick answered at once, "Do that. Look in the yellow pages. Find a priest and get him up here quickly. Please!" Silence.

"Mr. Dunn?" Roberta called.

Silence.

Roberta went to Rick's office door. She knocked on it. "Mr. Dunn?"

"Go away!" she heard.

"Do you still want that priest, Mr. Dunn?"

"I want you to go away, dammit!"

Roberta put her hand on the doorknob. Her stomach fluttered. "Perhaps a doctor, instead, sir?"

Silence.

Roberta added, "I can call Dr. Peterson for you. I can have him up here as quickly as possible." A short pause. "Do you think you need a doctor, Mr. Dunn?"

Silence.

Roberta's grip on the doorknob strengthened. Her stomach fluttered harder, as if there were some small bird inside her beating its wings. She smiled a flat, quivering smile and called, "I'm going to ring Dr. Peterson." She let go of the doorknob and added, "Unless you say otherwise, Mr. Dunn, I'm going to ring Dr. Peterson now and get him up here as quickly as possible."

Silence.

She turned, started for her desk, heard Rick's door being pulled open, glanced back.

She saw him coming at her, though so briefly that she was almost able to discount the whole thing with the flash of a smile and a breathy, "Oh?" as if he were playing a joke on her. He crossed the ten feet from his office door in only a second, and in the last bare fraction of that second, she realized what she was seeing, and knew that she was about to be slit open. She pitched wildly to her left, but her quick-wittedness was no match for his speed and agility. The blade entered her belly, just below her navel, and in her last moments, she thought that it was no more painful than a flu shot, that he had somehow miscalculated, only pricked her a little.

Five minutes after that, she had her intestines cupped in her dead hands, and Rick Dunn was wrapping her up in plastic.

"Is this Father Muldavey?"

"This is he."

"Father, I have a confession to make."

"Yes, of course. Please come to the confessional at six o'clock . . ."

"I don't have *time* for that. I want to make my confession *now*!"

A pause, then, "Are you Catholic?"

"That's a stupid question."

"Are you a member of my parish?"

"For Christ's sake, can't you simply—"

"Show some respect, please!"

"Why in the hell should I respect *you*? You're no one! You're just some asshole who's gotten himself possessed by the Holy Spirit. That can happen to anyone! I don't want to confess to *you*, I want to confess to *Him*, to *It*, to the Holy Spirit!"

"I'm afraid this conversation is growing very much out of hand—"

"You know what I've got in *my* hand, father? I've got a piece of rib cage in my hand! I broke it off the body of a woman I killed. I don't *want* to have a piece of a woman's rib cage in my hand, but it's there!"

"Clearly, my son, you are operating under a severe delusion."

"And clearly *you're* not listening to me. I have murder inside me, father. I'm confessing to you that I have murder inside me. Doesn't that matter to you?"

"My son, we all have murder inside us—"

"I don't need your fucking platitudes!"

The priest hung up.

"You know what I'm thinking, Rye?" asked Lenny. "I'm thinking that you're only halfway there when you say our murderer is an architect." They were in a small Italian restaurant on Bloor Street West, which was not far from Rick Dunn's office, though they weren't aware of it.

Ryerson said wearily, "Listen, the only reason I let you

come in here with me, Mr. Baker, was to tell you, once again, that we are not compatible—"

"No, really, Rye," Lenny cut in, and speared a piece of garlic-cheese bread with a fork. "I mean it." Ryerson rolled his eyes. Lenny continued, "Don't forget that I'm probably every bit as psychic as you are, and if we put our heads together, we can get this bastard!" He took a huge bite of the garlic-cheese bread and said as he chewed, "It's a woman, Rye. It's a woman architect who's missing a finger and wears purple lipstick." He swallowed, took another bite of the bread, and hurried on, "She's also a three-time divorcée—I mean, she's been married three times—"

"I knew what you meant, Mr. Baker."

"You can call me"—he swallowed—"Lenny. I wish you would. Anyway—hey, haven't we been waiting a long time for our spaghetti?"

"It's only been a few minutes, Mr. Baker." Ryerson sighed. He realized at last that it was going to be very, very hard indeed to free himself from this man. "Don't be impatient."

Lenny shrugged; his body shook. "Hey, I've always been impatient, Rye. It's in my blood. My father was impatient, and his father before him. I come from a long line of impatient people—we're all waiting for the world to catch up with us. And anyway, this woman, this three-time divorcée who wears purple lipstick and is missing a finger, is also a grandmother, even though she's only thirty-seven. I don't have her name yet, but I'm sure it will come to me in time."

"Yes," Ryerson said, "I'm sure it will."

Lenny's jaw fell open. His eyes widened; his face got red. "Great leaping ghosts!" he whispered. "*That's* her name! It's Juliet! Her name is Juliet!" He pushed himself heavily and awkwardly out of the chair. He began to growl.

"Stop that!" Ryerson whispered.

Lenny continued to growl.

Ryerson whispered, "What in the hell are you doing?"

Lenny stopped growling. He looked bewildered. He tilted his round pink head and said, "I'm sorry. What was I doing?"

"Sit down!" Ryerson ordered.

Lenny sat down. He leaned over the table. "Just tell me what I was doing, Rye."

"You know damned well what you were doing, Mr. Baker. And if it happens again—if you try to impress me with your . . . *sensitivity* again—"

"It wasn't an act." Lenny shook his head vehemently. "No, Rye, I swear to you that it wasn't an act."

Ryerson sighed. He was being unfair, he knew. After all, there had been plenty of times when *he'd* been an embarrassment to whomever he'd been with. He said, "You were growling."

Lenny's meaty brow furrowed. "No, I wasn't."

"Yes. You were. Just like Creosote." He stopped. "Damn!" he breathed. Creosote had been in the hotel room alone for a day and a half. Ryerson jumped to his feet. "Thanks, Lenny," he said and ran from the restaurant.

FOURTEEN

Lincoln Curtsinger was getting ready to teach his evening classes in Canadian literature at Toronto University when Rick Dunn came to his door. Lincoln was very conscientious about his teaching. He thought that although teaching wasn't the highest paid or the most prestigious of professions, it certainly was the noblest, and the most challenging; and it was from teaching, he maintained, that all other professions were made possible.

He was a slight, blotchy-skinned, timid man whose big, watery blue eyes seemed to betray a constant state of alert. For years, the inside of his mouth had been plagued by a strange purplish discoloration that his doctor had been unable to treat or even explain; so when he spoke, it was through a slit between his lips that was barely the width of a dime. He did not speak well this way—even though he'd been doing it for years—because his hearing was bad in the all-important mid-range, where the sound of voices occurs. He thought that his speech was impeccable and could not understand why people were constantly asking him to repeat himself.

He had grown to believe that the rest of the world was going deaf.

He said to Rick Dunn, who was grinning strangely at him outside Lincoln's Old York apartment, "Hullo, Rick. What is it you would like? I'm getting ready to go teaching in a few minutes."

And Rick said, "Teaching in a few minutes?" because that was all he had understood. "I won't be long. May I come in?"

Lincoln stepped aside. "Certainly, Rick, you may come in. Come in. I could make us some tea, but I have to go teaching in a few minutes."

Again, Rick understood clearly only the phrase "teaching in a few minutes," so he said, "I know," and stepped into the apartment.

Lincoln's apartment was a monument to books. There were books lining most of the walls, books on tables, books lying on chairs, and a few on the floor. And they were not just scholarly works. There were several hundred contemporary paperbacks of various genres, Westerns especially, which Lincoln had grown to love in the past five years. He liked to fantasize that he was a strong, lusty cowboy riding the American plains in search of gold, squaws, and gunfights. It was a fantasy he had cultivated because his psychologist had told him that fantasy was a terrific outlet for, as the psychologist had put it, "the constipated soul." Lincoln no longer felt constipated. He felt that he was living in several different worlds and so had one up on the rest of humanity. He said now to Rick, who had seated himself in a battered, overstuffed chair near the kitchen doorway, "I could get us some tea, but there is no time."

Rick said, "I came here, Lincoln, because you, of all people, can best appreciate what I have grown to be all about." His arms were flat on the arms of the chair. He was sitting very erect and still grinning strangely.

"Yes, good," said Lincoln, standing over him and smiling his pleasure that Rick would pay him such a compliment. "Thank you. And what is it about?"

Rick said, "It's about murder, Lincoln."

Lincoln clapped his tiny spidery hands and exclaimed, "Yes, murder *can* be fun, of course. What is it about murder?"

"Murder," Rick answered, "is power!"

Lincoln nodded. "Murder is the ultimate power!"

"The only power we have in life *is* life!" said Rick, thinking that Lincoln—of all his friends—could understand and appreciate what he was saying. "If we take away life, we take away power. We gather it unto ourselves, Lincoln. Tell me you understand that."

Lincoln said at once, although his voice trembled a little, as if it were on the verge of breaking, "Oh, yes, Rick. I do understand that."

"And," Rick hurried on, "we become like the great tiger in search of its prey. We become the benefactor to the weak because we take away misery. We become the keepers and maintainers of a healthy gene pool."

"Yes," said Lincoln, "I understand that, too."

"So, you see"—Rick cocked his head and shrugged—"that's why I'm here."

Lincoln's brow furrowed. "I *don't* understand that, Rick."

Rick put his hands palm down on the arms of the chair as if preparing to stand. "Do I really have to explain it, Lincoln?"

Lincoln thought only a moment, then answered, his voice trembling, "No, Rick, I don't think that you do."

Rick hadn't understood him. He said, "I'm sorry, Lincoln, you'll have to repeat that."

"Repeat what?"

"What you just said." Rick pushed himself to his feet quickly and powerfully. He was a good six inches taller than Lincoln, but at that moment, as Lincoln's mouth dropped open—revealing the purplish discoloration—and as his eyes widened in fear and anticipation, then as his thin, purplish red tongue stuck straight out because Rick's massive hands were hard on his throat, Rick might easily have been whole atmospheres taller, Rick might have been his personal God come down to exact payment for the gift of life. Which is precisely what Lincoln thought as death approached.

Then Rick, standing over Lincoln's small, thin body sprawled in the kitchen doorway, cocked his head in puzzlement, and said, "It's one possibility, Lincoln."

And he felt *people* crowding him, *people* pushing at him, *people* muttering all around him.

"The thing about possession," Ryerson said to Lenny as they walked on Yonge Street, "is that it splits the psyche into two parts, of course, and each part is vaguely aware of the other." He had Creosote in his arms and had vowed never to let him out of his sight again. Creosote's day-and-a-half alone in the hotel room had left both the room and the dog a mess. Ryerson had read an awful jumble of confusion, anger, anxiety, and depression in the dog and had realized then just how incredibly attached to the little soul he had become.

Lenny nodded. "I was possessed once." Ryerson had gotten him to change his stained white suit. He was wearing a pair of oversized gray pants ("From when I weighed thirty pounds more than I do now, Rye"), a brown silk shirt, ("I was into silk, once. You should see my tie collection"), and a huge blue overcoat that flopped to the right and left with each step.

Ryerson said, "No, Lenny. Please. Let's not start that, okay?"

Lenny looked crestfallen, but after a moment he brightened. "Sure, Rye. Sorry. Habit."

Ryerson went on. "And when people are possessed, they do things they wouldn't normally do—that is, the thing *possessing* them makes them do things they wouldn't normally do. And because the two halves are in communication with each other—albeit, weak communication—the things the person does while he's possessed are very, very troubling to his normal self. So he makes excuses for them. For himself. He begins to rationalize. I've seen it a dozen times, Lenny. And he rationalizes . . . the person being possessed rationalizes his behavior because he's caught up in the idea of ultimate responsibility. Society is, too. No matter *what* the reason for a crime, society demands punishment for it. For instance, society demands that a murderer who kills while under the duress of some insane compulsion be brought to justice *after* the insane compulsion has been eliminated, when the person has presumably become sane and responsible. It's the same sort of thinking that makes owners of antique shops put little signs up that say, 'You break it, you bought it.' Ultimate responsibility—because, after all, *someone's* got to take responsibility."

Yonge Street was crowded with chic, vivacious Torontonians. A dark-haired young woman walking toward them—she was dressed in a short brown leather skirt, frilly white blouse, and heavy black shawl—gave Lenny a very hungry and sensual look as she passed. Lenny's head turned. A huge, disbelieving grin broke out on his round, red face, and Ryerson said, "For instance, her."

"Her what?" said Lenny.

Ryerson smiled. "Why did she look at you the way she did, Lenny?"

Lenny shrugged. He was still grinning, but now he looked embarrassed, too. "She liked me, Rye."

Ryerson, regretting his words, at once, said, "Do you really believe that?"

Lenny's grin vanished. He looked hurt. He glanced quickly around again, and watched the woman turn the corner onto Bloor Street West. He said, looking back at Ryerson, "Why shouldn't I believe it? I'm not a virgin, you know. I've had more women than you can shake a stick at."

Ryerson transferred Creosote from one arm to the other. "Forget it," he said.

Lenny's red face got redder. "No, dammit—say what you were going to say."

Ryerson sighed. "I was simply going to ask whose responsibility it would have been if you'd gone to bed with her and gotten some . . . disease."

Lenny looked confused. He said, surprising Ryerson, "That's awfully . . . judgmental. That's"—he stopped, shook his head, repeated—"*awfully* judgmental!"

"Yes," Ryerson conceded. "I know it is. I'm sorry."

"I mean not just to me, Rye, but to her, too." He inclined his head backward.

Ryerson transferred the squirming Creosote from one arm to the other again and repeated, "Yes, I know. I'm sorry." It was the truth. His cruelty had made him feel like a jerk.

Lenny fumed, "You *should* be sorry, dammit!"

"It was simply to illustrate a point, Lenny."

"You don't make other people feel . . . *ugly,* just to illustrate a point."

"I didn't mean to make you feel ugly." Ryerson knew he was whining now. Once more he transferred Creosote to his other arm. This time the dog, in protest, raked his teeth along Ryerson's nose. Ryerson whispered, "Shit!" and felt his nose for blood. There was none.

"I'm just as much a person as *you* are!" Lenny proclaimed and suddenly veered away, crossed the street, and, in moments, disappeared in the crowds of beautiful Torontonians.

Ryerson said to Creosote, "Now I know what it feels like to make an ass of myself."

Creosote licked Ryerson's nose.

FIFTEEN

Max Tyler said to Dan Creed, "We got something here out of Chicago, Dan." Max had been born and raised in the States; he pronounced "out" as "out."

From behind his desk, Creed said, "Oh? What did you get out of Chicago?" He said "out" as "oot."

Max put a computer printout on Creed's desk. There was a computer-reproduced, low-resolution, black-and-white police photo at the top of the printout that showed what appeared to be a huge tube of plastic with the rough outline of a body visible within. The Cook County Medical Examiner's Report of Autopsy was printed beneath the photo, and, below that, two short paragraphs from the homicide lieutenant in charge of the investigation. At the bottom of the printout were the words: NO SUSPECTS—CASE OPEN.

Creed glanced over the two short paragraphs from the lieutenant in charge, then looked up at Tyler. "When did we get this?"

"Five minutes ago."

Creed smiled. "It's something, isn't it?"

"It's the same M.O.," Max said.

"Sure it's the same M.O. Our boy gets around. And because he gets around, Max, I think we can nail him." He picked up his phone, dialed. Seconds later, he reached the desk sergeant at the Eighth Precinct in Chicago, and seconds after that was connected with the homicide division. He said to the man who answered, "I'd like to speak with Lieutenant Sam Gears, please."

The man said, "The lieutenant's on assignment. Who's calling?"

Creed gave his name, quickly checked the computer printout, and asked, "Is George Ripley in?"

"Yes, he is," the man answered. "Hold on."

A moment later, Ripley came on the line. "Inspector Creed, this is Sergeant Ripley. What can I do for you?"

"I have a computer printout in front of me, sergeant, relative to an unsolved murder from"—he checked the date at the top of the printout—"eight years ago. A young woman named Augusta Mullen was the victim. She was stabbed, wrapped in plastic, and stuck up in a false ceiling in the Sears Tower. Do you remember the case?"

Ripley answered. "You bet I do."

"And do you have a file handy on it?"

"I don't have it handy, no, but I can get hold of it and call you back."

"Yes, thanks. I'll be here for another hour." He paused. "First, can you tell me what sorts of businesses there are in the Sears Tower?"

"What sorts of businesses? I'm not sure. Bankers, I think. And advertising agencies. Doctors' offices. Why?"

"There are probably lots of architects in there, wouldn't you say?"

"Probably. It's a damned big place, inspector."

"But you can't say for certain?"

"I can find out, if it's important." He paused. "You've had some trouble up there, haven't you?"

"Yes, we have." A pause. "Do you think you could get me a list of the architects in the Sears Tower at the time of the murder?"

Ripley said nothing for a moment, then: "I'm a little backed up with work here, inspector. I'd appreciate it if you could look into that yourself."

Creed sighed. "Sure. Okay. But call me back when you've pulled the file on that case, would you?"

"Will do."

Rick smiled a broad and ingratiating smile at Milly Farino when she opened her door for him. He said, "Well, hello, Milly. Can we talk?"

Milly, a short, thin woman, with long black hair, and a soft, inquiring look about her, had been interrupted as she was about to take her afternoon shower—she showered twice a day—had thrown a peach satin robe around herself and knotted it tightly. She gave him an uneasy smile and said, "I was about to shower, Rick." She thought it was strange that he was at her door. He had been there only once before, with a date, four months earlier, when Milly had thrown a cocktail party.

"I won't be long, Milly." Rick's smile grew broader and more ingratiating, which made Milly feel even more uneasy. She was an excellent reader of people, and she thought there was something odd about Rick today. She thought she was seeing two people instead of one—as if she were looking into an imperfectly glazed mirror, and there was a fuzzy, dark secondary image a couple of degrees to the left or right of the primary image. She lived in a suburban area five miles east of Toronto, in a small white Cape Cod that was one of a dozen small white, beige, or blue Cape Cods on the street. She glanced past Rick at his black Jaguar, parked on the street in front of the house. "You could have parked in the driveway, Rick," she said. "There's no parking on the street."

"Would you like me to move the car, Milly?" His ingratiating smile became inquiring.

She shook her head. "No. It will be okay for a minute or two, which, I'm afraid, is all I can spare you now." She backed away from the door and held it open. Rick walked past her, nodding, said, "Thanks, Milly," went into the tiny living room and sat cross-legged on a brown art deco love seat.

Milly stood in the living-room doorway, arms hanging in front of her stomach, hands clasped. She looked and felt on edge. "So, as I said, Rick, I can spare you just a few minutes—"

"Death really is the great equalizer, Milly."

She shook her head. "I'm sorry, Rick. Those are good cocktail-party lines, I suppose, but I really must ask you to get to the point."

"So you remember?"

"Of course I remember."

"Then the point is this, Milly: I always thought you were an elitist. I always thought you were a snob."

"Oh?"

"Yes, Milly."

Milly sniffed. The house was cool, and when she stood for too long dressed as she was now—in only a thin satin robe—her sinuses began to drain almost at once. "I see"—she gestured nervously with her arm—"you came here to tell me I'm a snob. Why, Rick?"

Rick stared at the floor, as if in thought. "It's not that I blame you, or ever blamed you, for being a snob. Some people are born fat. Some people are born thin. Some people are born snobs." He looked up at her. "Like you, Milly." He smiled again, but it was not ingratiating. It was flat and cruel.

"You came to my house merely to insult me, Rick?"

He said, ignoring her, "And even your house, Milly, is strangely elitist. It's so damned . . . humble. And you are so damned humble! And it's all so damned *false.* But death, ah yes, death"—he pointed straight into the air—"is indeed the great equalizer, just as you said. And I am merely the instrument of that . . . equalization." He chortled.

Milly took a quivering step backward, stopped, put her hand to her mouth, and sniffed again, deeply, so it sounded like a snort.

Rick said, "But *that* is so very real, Milly. *That* is real!" He pushed himself to his feet and wiped his hands together as if cleaning them.

"You're joking with me, Rick?" Milly asked.

He threw his big, square head back, glared at her down his nose, and pointed a stiff accusing finger at her. "Snob!" he bellowed. "Elitist! I am the great equalizer, and I have come to equalize!"

"Please say that you're only joking," Milly pleaded.

He shook his head. "No, I'm not," he bellowed. "I'm sorry. I'm not joking."

Milly backed up another step. Her robe slid open a little, revealing a thin pink thigh. "Are you going to rape me?"

"No." Rick smiled, as if at a bad joke. He was still pointing a stiff finger at her. "I don't want to rape you. I don't *need* to rape you, Milly Snob. I need to *murder* you!" And he was across the small room in a second.

"Inspector Creed, this is Sergeant Ripley in Chicago. I've got the file on the Augusta Mullen murder."

"Good. Thanks for calling back. There are some points I'd like to clear up—the computer printout I have is pretty sparse."

"Fire away."

"First of all, the plastic itself—"

"A polypropylene derivative. You can get it practically anywhere."

"So there was no probability of a lead there?"

"That's right."

"And the victim's fiancé?"

"Not a suspect."

"I see." Creed paused, then asked, "The victim's body was found on the ninety-sixth floor. Did it appear that that was where the murder took place?"

"We found absolutely no blood beyond what was on the inside of the plastic, Inspector. The murder could have taken place anywhere in that building."

"Did you work on the assumption that it took place on the ninety-sixth floor?"

"Why would we assume that, Inspector? We had no reason to assume anything."

"Merely as a starting point, sergeant."

"And if it hadn't panned out?"

"You'd have started somewhere else, of course." Creed found that he was losing his patience. He steadied himself. "I was merely wondering, sergeant, if you'd drawn up a list of the businesses on the ninety-sixth floor, and the ninety-fifth."

"Yes. The lieutenant—he was a sergeant then—had a list drawn up. You want it?"

"Can you read it to me?"

"Right now?"

"Yes, sergeant. If you don't mind."

"You got a pencil handy?"

"I'm recording our conversation."

"Okay, here we go. Wetterings and Agnew, Financial Advisors; Code, Boylan, Browne, and Doppler, Attorneys; Johnson and Taylor, Import-Export Bankers; Victor Technologies; Lawrence and Sharon McGovern, Tax Consultants." The list continued for another minute; then Ripley paused and asked, "You want the ninety-fifth floor now?"

"Do you mind?"

"It'd be easier to send it to you."

"And it would take longer, I'm afraid. Please read it."

"It's your ear." He continued reading for another minute, then ended with "Yaeger, Svenson and Trumbley."

Creed broke in, "Could you give me the name of that architect again?"

"Sure, 'Yaeger, Svenson and Trumbley.' Does that mean something to you?"

"Can you find out if they're still in the building?"

"I can give you the number for the Sears Tower Management Association and you can call them yourself, Inspector."

Creed noted more than a hint of weariness in Ripley's voice. "Yes, thank you. I'll do that."

Ripley gave him the number.

"You have a man staying here whose name is Baker," Ryerson Biergarten said to the desk clerk at the Brownstone Hotel on King Street. "Can you tell me his room number, please."

The desk clerk shook his head slowly. "I'm sorry, sir, but I can't give you that information without a warrant or permission from the party himself."

"But he *is* staying here?"

"Information as to the identity of our guests, sir, is strictly confidential without, as I've said—"

"Room 412?"

The desk clerk's mouth dropped open.

"Thanks," Ryerson said and went to the elevators.

"Yaeger, Svenson and Trumbley, Architects," cooed the receptionist.

Dan Creed identified himself and said, "Could I speak with Mr. Yaeger, Mr. Svenson, or Mr. Trumbley, please."

The receptionist answered, "It's *Ms.* Svenson, sir, and I'm sorry, but neither she nor the other partners are in at the moment. Perhaps I could help you."

"Perhaps." Creed paused. He wasn't sure what he was looking for. He wasn't entirely convinced that he wasn't barking up the wrong tree by following through on what Ryerson Biergarten had said. He went on, "How long have you been working in the Sears Tower?"

"Ten years."

"So you'd have a good idea of the businesses that have come and gone from there in that time?"

"No, sir. It's a very big building."

"I understand that. I'm talking specifically about architectural firms—"

"There are ten architectural firms in the Sears Tower, Mr. Creed."

"And has that remained fairly constant?"

"Yes. People come and go, but the old, established firms, such as ours, remain."

Creed smiled. "You wouldn't know just how many architectural firms have come and gone in the past five or six years, would you?"

"I wouldn't have that information right at my fingertips, no." She paused. "Please hold, I have another call." Moments later, she came back on the line. "As I was saying, sir, I wouldn't have that information right at my fingertips. However, the Sears Tower Management Association would. I have their number—"

"Yes, so do I. Thanks." He paused, then hurried on, before she hung up, "Miss? One more thing?"

"Yes?"

"Has your firm ever employed any junior partners—architects who wouldn't be on your masthead, I mean."

"I know what you mean, sir. Yes, we have. Since I have been with the firm, we've employed eight junior partners."

"Are they all still with the firm?"

"All but three, sir."

"Could you give me their names?"

"Sir, they were killed in a plane crash four years ago."

"Oh. Sorry."

"We also had a fourth partner. A senior partner. He's no longer with the firm. He left us five years ago."

"And his name?"

"Fredrick Dunn."

"Could you spell that?"

She did. Creed went on, "And where did he go?"

"I'm not sure. I think that he left the state." She paused. "I'm not at all sure that he didn't leave the country."

Creed had gotten the Toronto yellow pages from a bottom drawer of his desk as soon as she'd given him the name Fredrick Dunn, and he had turned hurriedly to ARCHITECTS. Now a little whoop of joy escaped him.

In Chicago, the receptionist at Yaeger, Svenson and Trumbley said, "Sorry, sir?"

"Do you believe in miracles?"

"Not really."

Creed said, "Well, *I* do!"

SIXTEEN

Ryerson pleaded, "One of my major imperfections, Lenny, is that I can be a real bastard!"

Lenny had opened his hotel-room door only part way and was scowling at Ryerson. "I don't *need* you, Rye! I don't need your crap!"

Ryerson shifted the squirming Creosote so he was up on his shoulder and facing backward. Ryerson nodded. "I agree, Lenny. And if you decide to simply slam the door in my face, I'll understand. However, I came here for two reasons."

Lenny's scowl softened.

Ryerson continued, "I came here, first of all, to apologize for what I said. It was cruel and stupid."

"I agree," Lenny whispered tightly.

"And I came here, also, because I need your help."

Lenny's soft scowl disappeared. It was replaced by a quick, incredulous smile. Then the scowl returned. "Why the hell would you need *my* help?"

"Because," Ryerson answered, his tone hard and serious, "I'm trying to catch a murderer, and I think I can do it more quickly if both of our brains are working on it."

Lenny's scowl disappeared. He smiled again, broadly, incredulously. "Didn't I tell you, Rye? Didn't I tell you?"

"Tell me what, Lenny?" Ryerson was smiling, too. He was pleased with Lenny's happiness.

"That we're a team. Didn't I tell you that?"

Ryerson nodded. Creosote belched. Ryerson said, "Yes, I believe you did."

Rick Dunn said to the waitress at Lorenzo's Restaurant on Queen Street, "I need a priest."

The waitress quipped, "If it's not on the menu, we don't have it." She smiled. Her smile vanished under Rick's cold, hard gaze.

He said in a stiff monotone, "I'm going to eat here, Miss. And when I'm done, I'm going to go and find a priest. A Roman Catholic priest. And what I'm asking you is this: is there a Roman Catholic church nearby?"

The waitress shrugged. "So who goes to church?" She glanced at another waitress working the front part of the small restaurant. "I'll ask Freda." She paused. "What are you going to have?"

Rick studied the menu a few moments then asked, "How's the vegetable lasagna?"

"The vegetable lasagna's real good. You want some?"

Rick nodded. "Yes, thank you. Plus a glass of milk, please. And a side order of whole-wheat toast."

"Sure," said the waitress. "I'll ask Freda about that church."

"It's urgent," said Rick.

* * *

"Possessed people," Ryerson explained as Lenny got into his freshly laundered white suit, "are still the people that they always were. That's important. And, as I said before, the psyche becomes split into two unequal halves that are in communication with each other—which is to say that each half knows that the other half exists, although this knowledge can be on a very elemental, very instinctive level.

"Possession, Lenny, can also release us from the constraints that civilization imposes on our normal psyches. When we're possessed, we may experience feelings that we have never experienced before, and those feelings may be very pleasurable." He stopped; Lenny had disappeared into a walk-in closet.

Lenny called, "Yeah, I'm listening."

Ryerson put Creosote on the floor. The dog looked momentarily confused, then trotted across the room and tore into one of Lenny's saddle shoes. Ryerson breathed, "Oh, hell!" vaulted across the room, and yanked the shoe from Creosote's mouth.

Lenny reappeared. "What's going on, Rye?"

Ryerson grinned sheepishly, glanced at the saddle shoe in his right hand, then at Creosote in his left, and said, looking at Lenny, "Creosote was eating your shoe. I'm sorry."

"My saddle shoe?"

"Yes." Ryerson held up the shoe. "But it's okay. I got to him in time."

"Saddle shoes aren't easy to come by, you know."

Ryerson nodded. Creosote strained hard to get another bite of the shoe. "I'm aware of that, Lenny. And they're very nice shoes."

Lenny had his white suit jacket in hand. He said as he poured himself into it, "You're patronizing me, Rye. I wish you wouldn't. You think saddle shoes are stupid—admit it."

Ryerson considered, then shook his head. "They're not stupid, Lenny. Whatever someone wants to wear is *his* business. Look at me. My first wife said I had the 'poor man's preppy look,' and I guess she was right."

Lenny crossed the room, took the saddle shoe from Ryerson, and sat on the bed to put it on. "Everyone's got his particular costume," he said.

Ryerson said, "You continually astound me, Lenny."

"Can I speak plainly, Father?"

"You may speak whatever is in your heart, my son. How long has it been since your last confession?"

"Twenty-five years."

"That's a very long time."

"Is that a joke?"

"No, it's not a joke, merely an observation."

"I have murder in my heart, Father."

"Which is to say—"

"Which is to say that I've killed a few people—one or two or three people."

The priest gasped.

"Good," Rick said. "You believe me. The last asshole I talked to thought I was being . . . allegorical."

The priest said, his tone forced, and his voice dry, "This is a very, very serious thing you have confessed, and though I am duty bound to—" There was a knock at the door to his side of the confessional. "Who is it?"

"Sister Felicia."

"Yes, what is it, Sister?"

"Someone has fainted in the chancel, Father."

"Then see to him."

"It's a woman, Father. And I can't rouse her. I've called for an ambulance."

"What do you mean you can't rouse her?"

"She will not come around, Father. I felt that you should be told immediately."

The priest said nothing.

Rick chuckled.

The priest turned his gaze to the screen that separated him from Rick and whispered hoarsely, "What have you done?"

Rick answered, "Only what gives me pleasure. You know, Father, it's what life's all about." The priest shot from his side of the confessional and ran toward the chancel. Rick rattled on, mindless of the fact that he was speaking to himself, "I asked someone once, half-jokingly, 'What's life all about?' And this person answered, 'My Zen master said Life is like a ship that goes out on the great ocean.' I looked at her. I thought she was going to give me some pseudospiritual bullcrap. But she continued, 'The ship is going to sink eventually, and you can either have a great time before that happens, or you can have a lousy time. But,' she emphasized, 'it *is* going to sink.' So, Father, before my ship sinks, I'm going to have one hell of a time!"

*   *   *

Max Tyler said to Inspector Creed, "There's no answer at this guy's office, Dan."

Creed checked his watch. It was 2:30 on a Tuesday afternoon. "Someone should be there," he said. "His secretary, anyway."

"That's what I thought," Tyler said.

Creed stood up, got his coat from a coatrack near his desk and headed for the door. Max stepped out of his way. Creed said as he passed, "We're going over there, Max."

"Sure thing."

Creed stopped and put his hand on Max's shoulder. "Call Ryerson Biergarten, would you? Have him meet us there."

"Where's he staying?"

Creed looked confused. "Damn, I don't know." He shook his head. "Forget it—let's get over to this guy's office. If Biergarten is all he claims to be, he'll be there waiting for us."

At that moment, Ryerson was walking on King Street with Lenny Baker, and he was delivering a monologue. He was also feeling a twinge at the nape of his neck, as if some small creature had begun burrowing into his skin. It felt like the combination of a dull ache and a soft itch, and while he delivered his monologue, he tried to figure out what the twinge was telling him. "So you see my point, don't you, Lenny?"

Lenny nodded uncertainly.

Ryerson hurried on, "I'll simplify it—"

Lenny scowled at him.

"Sorry," Ryerson said and meant it. He continued, "Let's say that . . . that Creosote, here,"—up on his shoulder and looking backward—"became possessed by the spirit of a pit bull. If that happened, it would be reasonable to expect that he would, at times, *act* like a pit bull, right? He'd have the soul of a killer." He paused. The twinge at the nape of his neck was growing stronger. He continued, "And the point is, Lenny—Creosote already *has* the soul of a killer. Like all dogs, he's descended from wolves. So if he became possessed by the spirit of a pit bull, well, then, it would probably go a long way toward awakening the wolf buried deep somewhere in his psyche."

Lenny pursed his lips. "That little dog might have a *brain,* Rye, but it sure as hell ain't got a *psyche!*"

Ryerson grimaced.

Lenny gave him a puzzled look. "You okay?"

Ryerson shook his head again. "I don't think so." Arms trembling, he took Creosote down from his shoulder and held him out to Lenny. "Take him, would you? I've got to sit down."

"Sure." Lenny took Creosote. "What's the matter, Rye? Tell me what's wrong." He began to feel the same sort of twinge that Ryerson was feeling.

Ryerson sat on the front steps of the Ox Cart Bookstore. A woman came out of the store as he sat down. She stood watching him because he was in her way. After a few moments, Lenny bent over and said, "Rye, this woman wants to get by."

Ryerson nodded once, head in his hands, but didn't move.

"Does he have a problem?" the woman asked. She was round faced and gray haired, dressed for an evening on the town, and she looked as if she spent much of her time smiling. She was smiling now, a smile of concern.

"I can dance," Ryerson whispered.

The woman asked, "Did he say he wants to dance?"

But now the twinge at the nape of Lenny's neck had become nearly as severe as Ryerson's. He put his hand over it while he clutched the squirming Creosote hard to his chest, and grimaced.

"Good Lord!" the gray-haired woman muttered.

Lenny plopped down next to Ryerson on the front step of the Ox Cart Bookstore. The gray-haired woman stopped smiling. "Perhaps," she suggested, "you could both find somewhere *else* to sit." Her smile reappeared, then vanished. "Somewhere not quite so *public*!"

Ryerson moaned, "I can dance, I can dance!"

Lenny simply moaned.

Creosote belched and snorted in protest at being held so tightly against Lenny's chest.

The gray-haired woman opened and closed her mouth several times, in rapid succession, then went back into the bookstore. Moments later, she reappeared with the store's manager in tow and pointed a stiff finger at Ryerson and Lenny. "These two, Mr. Kilodney!"

The store manager, a tall, soft-faced, pleasant-looking young man whose first name was Crad, came forward and tapped Ryerson on the shoulder. "I'm sorry, sir—"

"I can dance!" Ryerson shouted.

Crad Kilodney jumped backward in surprise, arms

akimbo. His elbow connected solidly with the brick wall of the entranceway, and he yelped in pain.

The gray-haired woman announced, "Well, now, *this* is getting very much out of hand!"

In an office building on Bloor Street West, Max Tyler was trying hard to keep his lunch down.

Creed said, "You want to leave, Max? It's okay."

Max nodded, then stumbled, hand to his stomach, from Rick Dunn's office. Creed was surprised. Max had seen quite a lot in his ten years working homicide. Perhaps, Creed thought, it was the smell in here, like the smell of a slaughterhouse.

He set to work.

What remained of Roberta's body was on its back on top of Rick's desk, arms and legs wide, the trunk reduced to a reddish brown jumble of internal organs, the mouth and eyes opened halfway, as if Roberta were at the edges of sleep. She wore a pleated gray skirt and white blouse, although they existed only as shredded masses at the top of her chest and around her knees. Between those points, the cloth had become an integral part of her internal organs, as if rust-colored cardboard had erupted from her lungs, her heart, her stomach.

Creed left Rick's office, went to the phone on Roberta's desk, took a handkerchief from his pocket, cupped it in his hand, and picked up the receiver. He called the desk sergeant at his precinct house, told him to get out an APB on Rick Dunn, was asked for a description, and said he'd get one soon. Then he called the medical examiner, the forensics unit, and was about to call out to Max Tyler, whom he assumed was just beyond the office door, when Rick Dunn came in.

He stopped a few feet inside the entranceway. "Who are *you*?" he said, looking very surprised.

Creed answered, "Are you Fredrick Dunn?"

Rick shook his head. "No, no. You just tell me who in the hell you are, and what you're doing here—"

"Mr. Dunn, my name is Inspector Dan Creed." He took his shield from his jacket pocket, held it out for Rick to see, then put it back in his pocket. "Are you Fredrick Dunn?"

Rick said, "Has something happened here?"

"Mr. Dunn, perhaps you'd like to speak with an attorney."

Rick shook his head. "Tell me what has *happened* here, dammit!"

"There's been a murder, sir, and there are some questions I would—"

"Who?"

"Apparently, it's your secretary, Mr. Dunn."

"Roberta?" A quivering smile appeared on Rick's face. "Someone murdered Roberta?"

"Is that her name, sir? Could I have her last name, please?"

"My name isn't Fredrick Dunn. It's Giuseppe Balboa."

This took Creed aback. "I'm sorry," he said. "Your name is *what*?"

Rick went on, smiling cordially, "I'm a friend of Mr.

Dunn's. I've worked with him. We are fellow architects."
He put his right hand into the pocket of his overcoat.

Creed said, "Take your hand out of your pocket!"

Rick shrugged. "I have nothing in here." He kept his hand in his pocket.

Creed's hand went to the .38 in his shoulder holster. He called, "Max, come in here!"

Rick said, "Who's Max?"

Creed's hand closed on the grip of his .38. He called again, "Max, dammit, come in here!"

Rick said, moving one step closer to Creed, "Is Max the husky fellow in the hallway?" He moved another step closer.

Creed pulled his .38 out and pointed it at Rick. "Stop right there!"

Rick smiled broadly. He shook his head. "As I told you, I have nothing in my pocket." He took his hand from his pocket and held it out, palm up. "See. Nothing."

Creed snapped, "Over there!" and jerked the gun to indicate the wall.

Rick said, "Over where?" His hand went into his pocket again.

"Now!" Creed ordered.

Rick inclined his head downward obliquely, as if ready to do what Creed was ordering him to do. Then his hand came out of his pocket again.

SEVENTEEN

The very last thought in Inspector Dan Creed's head was *Shit! This is something supernatural!* He had never believed in the supernatural. He had believed in telepathy because he had seen Ryerson at work, but he had never believed in spirits, which, as far as he was concerned, were the bulwark of the "world of the supernatural." And he had never believed in demons, or possession, which, also as far as he was concerned, were Hollywood concoctions. But at that moment, as he thought, *Shit! This is something supernatural!*—as he held the .38 pointed at Rick Dunn's chest—he knew that a haphazard assumption he had carried through life was tragically incorrect.

He saw two faces in the space where only one face should have been. He saw Rick Dunn's face—flat, broad and large nosed, wide mouth, small, straight teeth, and hazel eyes nearly puffed shut by what he had supposed was lack of sleep. And he saw another face superimposed upon it. The face of a man twenty years younger than Rick Dunn, whose smooth reddish skin was stretched tight because the young mouth was open as if in a scream, and the blue eyes were wide and disbelieving and terrified.

Rick Dunn feinted to his right a fraction of a second before Creed got off a shot, and the slug tore into the door frame.

Then, with the strength and speed of the two men he was at that moment, Rick Dunn shoved the long, heavy screwdriver hard into Dan Creed's gut and yanked upward, pulling the blade through Creed's breastbone and tearing his heart apart within a second.

And in the moment before death overtook him, Creed saw this, too: He saw *people* clustered around his murderer, and darkness around them, and he got a sense of *place,* and of *altitude,* and *hunger.*

At that moment, Ryerson Biergarten, still sitting on the front step of the Ox Cart Bookstore on King Street, cut loose with a scream of pain so piercing and abrupt that a young man walking by looked over, startled, and slammed into a middle-aged woman walking her Pekingese. The woman went over backward. The man went down on top of her. The Pekingese yelped and because the woman, in her fall, had dropped the leash, tore off down King Street. Creosote—who had managed to squirm out of Lenny Baker's arms—tore off in hot pursuit.

Then Lenny Baker screamed. Not for the same reason that Ryerson had screamed, but *because* Ryerson had screamed. Ryerson screamed again. Lenny screamed again. The middle-aged woman with the young man on top of her pushed desperately and ordered, in a coarse low voice, "Get off me, you naughty boy!"

Ryerson launched himself from the step and began running in the direction that Creosote had run. But he wasn't running after Creosote. Although he didn't know it, he was running toward Rick Dunn.

Lenny screamed again, then pushed himself up awkwardly, and lumbered after Ryerson.

When he looked at himself, Max Tyler did not want to be alive. He saw his intestines dangling down his left side to the floor. He saw what he thought was either his spleen or his bladder bulging to the right of his intestines. Then, though he had never been a religious man, he began to mumble a prayer: "God, let me die, let me die!" because he knew that he was going to die anyway, and he thought it would be better when someone happened upon him if he were already dead. Then he wouldn't have to endure that person's panic, desperation and, at last, the stupid and pleading reassurances that he—Max—would be "all right." Max had given the same kind of reassurances two dozen or more times in his years as a cop. The first time was with a young shotgun-blast victim who was missing half his head and yet still, miraculously, clung to life. "Am I all right?" he asked Max gurglingly. "Am I okay?"

And Max had told him, smiling a little, "Sure you are. You're fine. You'll be home in no time." The young man died moments later, and Max couldn't help wondering if, at the last moment, he had resented Max, even cursed him silently, for his false reassurance. Max could think of nothing worse than being the brunt of the last curse of the dying.

He saw someone come around the corner of the hallway. He felt his arm move for the .45 he kept in his shoulder holster, felt his hand grip the weapon, felt himself draw it, aim it, heard himself bark, "Stop right there!" It was conditioning that gave him this fantasy, of course. He said nothing. His body lay still. His breathing grew shallower by the moment. Death was only moments away.

Ryerson Biergarten bent over him, put a hand on his shoulder. "My God," Ryerson said, "I'm sorry."

Max Tyler managed a very small smile. Then he whispered, "No problem. Thanks." And, as his spirit drifted off, Ryerson grabbed several images from him:

The image of Rick Dunn. And the image of the younger man screaming inside Rick Dunn.

And the image of a multitude shouldering closer and still closer. The image of darkness. The sense of altitude.

And the image of Max moving through it. The image of Max, the spirit, Max *himself* ascending with such beauty and such grace. The end of life was clearly the beginning of life.

"Freeze!" Ryerson heard from behind him.

Rick Dunn stood very still in one corner of a service elevator that served the west side of his building. He was adding up his choices. He knew he was in trouble. He knew his life had taken an abrupt turn. He knew that he would no longer be able to be the same man he had been a month before: the Rick Dunn who went to bed late and got up early and, two or three times a week, shared his bed with someone he'd picked up at a singles bar. The Rick Dunn who wrote his mother in Chicago a long and newsy letter once a month, and got, once a month, a short letter in return which said, in essence, *Thank you, son. You help ease my pain.* The Rick Dunn who, several years earlier, had been at the top of his profession, who'd even been asked to send a bio to *Who's Who.* The Rick Dunn who liked to speed over the back roads twenty miles from Toronto in his black Jaguar simply for the thrill of it.

The Rick Dunn who had always, even as a child, had a strange fascination with death and with murder, but who had been able to keep it at arm's length, like some perverse fantasy he took out and studied only in his private moments.

Now all that had changed. His life had taken an abrupt turn because he had realized at last that what had been a fantasy was really a power demanding to be let out, an authority ordering him to give it free rein. It was clearly something *divine,* and how could he argue with that?

But now he had to protect it. And that meant protecting himself.

He couldn't go home, he realized. Those who sought to usurp his divine authority over the lives of the deficient (and who were disguised variously as police, building inspectors, and even as people on architectural planning committees) would be waiting for him. He couldn't go to his country home, either. They knew about his country home by now, and they'd be waiting there, too. He could check into a hotel, of course. And, of course, he'd have to use a different name.

A janitor got on the service elevator, then. He had a toolbox in one hand and a cup of coffee in the other. He was in his late sixties, thin, with a great mop of uncombed white hair. He was also nearly blind, so when Rick shook his head angrily at him, the janitor gave a cordial nod, stepped to the other side of the elevator, leaned over, and peered hard at the floor buttons. He knew most of them by touch and could press any floor from the first to the eighteenth without looking. But today he was going to the roof to spend some time with an aging cold-air vent that needed repair. "Spending time" with whatever needed his attention was all that he had been able to do since his eyesight began to fail several years earlier.

He glanced around at Rick. He saw him only as a large grayish lump and he knew, from the general shape of the lump, and also from the heavy, earthy smell coming from it, that it was male. He smiled, nodded cordially again, and said, "The roof?"

Rick said nothing.

The janitor said, "The roof button?"

Rick shook his head vehemently. The janitor did not see this well; but, having witnessed the same gesture many times before, knew what it was and continued his close inspection of the floor buttons. He smiled sweetly as he looked. He was a contented man because he had purpose in life.

He set his toolbox down and homed in with a stiff finger on a likely-looking button. He saw it light up when he pressed it, and it was like the sudden appearance of a bright full moon in the darkness. His sweet smile grew broad. He picked up his toolbox, straightened, and turned to face the elevator doors; their closing would be another small event in his life—like the lighting of the elevator button—although he wouldn't so much see it as feel and hear it.

The successful punching of the elevator button and the anticipation of the closing of the doors had made him forget about the large gray lump that was Rick. So when he saw two lumps side by side, he thought that it might be good to say something—the service elevator was, after all, a limited-use elevator. But then the doors closed, and his new anticipation became reaching the roof and "spending time" with the cold-air vent. He nodded at the two gray lumps—one thinner and taller than the other—and said, "Going up now."

"I can dance," said one of the lumps.

This dismayed the janitor; not only because it seemed a strange thing to say at that moment, but also because the voice that had said it was warbling and strained, like the voice of a man-sized insect.

The elevator lurched upward. Some of the janitor's coffee sloshed out onto his hand, but it was only lukewarm, so he merely set his toolbox down again and swiped at the spill with his other hand.

He felt suddenly as if he were closed in with two angry animals. He felt crowded, pushed on all sides, as if there were dozens of people packed into the elevator. It was a feeling so intense that his body stiffened.

*   *   *

Lenny Baker knew that he had trespassed into a world that was alien to him. He had never before felt so very alone and so confused.

It was a world that he had followed Ryerson into and now was trapped in.

It would have been okay—it would have been better, at least—if there was not so much here that was familiar. If this world were totally unlike his own, then he could dismiss it as craziness.

But this world was real.

There, far ahead at the horizon, was the great shaft of the CN Tower. Around him, the glass and steel monoliths that comprised the heart of Toronto. And moving purposefully past him, the chic, attractive, smiling Torontonians.

But between the buildings, around the phallic thrust of the tower, snaking past the chic and attractive Torontonians was that . . . presence.

He could think of no other word for it. He did not want to think of another word for it. He had strength and will enough merely to witness it, to let his senses record it.

He realized at once that it was something which had always been available for his senses to record, that there had even been moments—in his childhood, especially—when he had witnessed it. But most of those moments had been fleeting and quickly forgotten, like the moment when something very tasty first passes over the tongue.

Once, in his mid-teens, that moment had lasted longer, and he had stood openmouthed in awe of it. His Uncle Lucius had been with him.

"Tell me what you're seeing," Uncle Lucius had coaxed.

Lenny could only shake his head.

"Lift your hand up," said Uncle Lucius.

Lenny lifted his hand slowly, as if it were very heavy.

"Now," said Uncle Lucius, when Lenny's hand was poised at the horizontal, "touch."

Then the moment ended.

Lenny looked quizzically at Uncle Lucius. Again he shook his head. "I . . . I don't . . ."

Uncle Lucius said, "You have seen all there *is* to see. I want you to describe it."

"I can't . . . I don't know how . . ."

Uncle Lucius nodded. "I understand," he said.

Lenny wished now that Uncle Lucius were here so he could explain to him what his own phrase—"All there *is* to see"—really meant.

The presence.

A phrase came to Lenny as he witnessed it. It was a phrase that had been drilled into him by his tenth-grade American history teacher ("Have you got that now, Mr. Baker? Have you *got* that now?")

That phrase was *E pluribus unum. Out of the many, one.*

Because the presence, *this* presence had been generated by all the chic, attractive, smiling Torontonians, and by him, and by the dying, the old, the just-born and the about-to-be-born. It bound them together. They made it. They shared it. It was like the air that moved from here to there, got inhaled and exhaled, exchanged, changed, and changed again.

E pluribus unum.

It was from all of them, and it bound them together.

It was their nakedness. It was *themselves.* It moved around them and through them like a fog.

It was all there was to see.

"And that's *all* you know, Mr. Biergarten?" barked Chief Inspector Marion Erik. He was a tall, rotund, bald man who rarely smiled. He was scowling now. On his round red face it looked like the caricature of a scowl painted on a basketball. He added, "For God's sake, what in the hell did we hire you for?"

"You didn't hire me," Ryerson said. He was seated on an overstuffed red leather chair in a lounge on the first floor of Rick's building. For most of the conversation, Chief Inspector Erik had been seated in a chair near him, but as the questioning proceeded, it had been clear to Ryerson that the inspector's agitation and frustration was growing more and more acute. Finally the man had thrown himself from the chair and taken up a position in front of Ryerson, feet apart, body bent slightly forward, hands thrust hard into the pockets of his gray suit pants, where he clenched and unclenched his fists. He shook his head. "What kind of *psychic* are you? Hell, *we* know more than you do."

"I've got to find my dog." Ryerson's tone was hard, his pitch slightly off-key.

"Your *dog*? What the hell does your dog have to do with these murders, Mr. Biergarten?"

"Nothing." Ryerson kept his eyes straight ahead, so his gaze was between Inspector Erik's knees. "But he's my dog, and I love him, and he's lost somewhere in the city."

"And so is the asshole who chopped up two of my best detectives!" bellowed the chief inspector.

Ryerson looked up at him and cocked his head. "You have the man's name. It's Fredrick Dunn. He works in this building. He's an architect—"

Erik cut in, turning sideways to Ryerson and pointing stiffly at the door. "You can go! I *want* you to go! You've been an embarrassment to the city and to this police department for too damned long. My God, I wish I had the authority to order you out of Toronto."

Ryerson looked at him, head still cocked, for several moments. Then he stood up and moved stiffly past him, toward the door. When he was halfway there, the chief inspector called, "What I *can* do, Mr. Biergarten, and what I am *going* to do is get a court order barring you from talking to any of the principals in this case. I should have that accomplished by the evening."

Ryerson stopped. He glanced back. He said, barely above a whisper, "I don't need to *talk* to anyone, Inspector." Then he turned and left the building.

EIGHTEEN

Chief Inspector Erik was standing in the doorway to Rick Dunn's office after the bodies of Max Tyler, Dan Creed, and Roberta Shiffren had been taken to the morgue, and was saying to himself that Canada was going to hell in a handbasket, when a uniformed officer tapped him on the shoulder and said, "Sir? Someone to talk to you."

The inspector turned, blinked, and said, "Who?"

The uniformed cop nodded to indicate a tall, thin man with a mop of white hair who was standing in the doorway to the outer office. The officer explained, "It's the janitor."

"What's he want?"

"He says someone frightened him, sir. He wanted to report it."

Inspector Erik went over to the janitor, who smiled and bent his head forward, as if to see better, then stuck his hand out. The inspector shook it and asked, "What can I do for you?"

"Men in the elevator," the janitor said and stopped smiling. His voice was a surprisingly strong tenor.

"What about them?" asked the inspector.

The janitor nodded. "They weren't supposed to be there."

"I see." The inspector wanted a quick end to this conversation. "Perhaps you could give that information to your superior, whoever he may be."

"They were evil men!" the janitor declared.

The inspector wasn't impressed. He said anyway, "And what did they do that caused you to believe they were evil?"

"They made the elevator burn!" the janitor answered.

"What do you mean they made the elevator burn?"

"It's what they did!" the janitor cried.

"When was this?"

"An hour ago. It was an hour ago."

The inspector glanced around at the cop. "What do you know about this?"

"Nothing, sir. It's the first I've heard of it."

The inspector looked at the janitor. "Can you take this officer to the elevator you're talking about, please?" he asked. The janitor nodded enthusiastically.

And now, at dusk, the *presence* was a moving, slithering, dancing luminescence, airy and ghostlike.

Lenny Baker didn't know where his feet had taken him. The *presence* was its own pathway.

He had blundered across streets against traffic lights, had plunged through crowds of Torontonians, and now he was following one particular pathway that the *presence* had created for him. He didn't know where it would lead, and he followed it in response to his psychic sense, which he had never been able to define or control.

Now that psychic sense had exploded, and it was why he was seeing what he was seeing—the *presence,* the luminescence snaking through the city, linking all its living things.

It was a *part* of them, it was *from* them, *because* of them—like ten million phone calls over ten million telephone lines laid down randomly on the countryside. And Lenny knew which line to follow.

Though he didn't know why, or to what it might lead.

Ryerson Biergarten was trying to tune in to Creosote. He was aware that there were far more pressing issues at hand, that the ultimately moral thing to do would be to forget his Boston Bull terrier and concentrate on finding Fredrick Dunn.

But that was something that scared the hell out of him. He knew as graphically and as clearly as Fredrick Dunn himself the power the man possessed, and it was a power that Ryerson was not enthusiastic to challenge—though challenge it he must. In time.

He was near the corner of Bloor Street West and Queen Street, in the Yorkville district of Toronto. A breeze had come up and the air was growing chilly. He was standing still, trying hard to get some sense of Creosote, but was having no luck.

As a point of focus, he was using a mannequin dressed in a black evening gown. The mannequin was facing him from a shop window across the street. Next to the mannequin sat a life-size ceramic representation of a long-muzzled white dog with black spots. The dog's head was pointed toward the mannequin. On the other side of the mannequin, a male mannequin sat in a beige wing chair with his legs crossed and a pipe in his mouth. He was wearing a purple robe, gray slacks, and slippers, and his gaze was on Ryerson.

The dog turned its head and looked at Ryerson. At first Ryerson didn't notice because his concentration was on the female mannequin. But after a few moments, the visual information—that something just outside his circle of focus had changed—got through to his brain, and he looked at the dog. It had no expression. Its black-and-white ceramic eyes were half-closed, and its long mouth was open partway, so the suggestion of a light pink tongue was visible within.

The dog stood. For several moments, its large, lean body—like the body of a greyhound but with the coloring of a dalmatian—stayed still. Then quickly, with sure, fluid grace, it leaped through the plate-glass window without shattering it, turned left, and loped north on Queen Street.

Ryerson followed, his stride as long and as graceful as the dog's. He knew that eventually he would need to cross Queen Street; perhaps, he decided, when he reached Yonge.

He was running very fast (in college, he'd been a champion long-distance runner) and skillfully dodging people while keeping his eye on the ceramic dog moving swiftly down the well-lighted street.

Suddenly the dog veered west down an alley. Ryerson

glanced left quickly, then right. The street was clear. He vaulted across it after the dog and into the alley.

He stopped.

The dog was nowhere in sight.

He peered behind at the street, then back into the alley. Nothing. "Hell!" he breathed. These runners, as he thought of them, were so damned unreliable—lose sight of them for just a moment, and . . .

A flash of white appeared at the end of the alleyway. He riveted his gaze on it. It was the dog. It turned right, so it was once again heading north—on York Street, now—and was gone. Ryerson ran after it. He knew that if it stayed out of his sight for very long, his psychic connection with it would end, and he'd be back to square one.

"Inspector Erik?" said the uniformed cop.

The inspector turned from the window in Fredrick Dunn's office. "Yes?" He saw that the janitor was standing with the uniformed cop, who looked confused, gestured toward the door, and said, "It's a very strange thing, sir. Perhaps you should come and see it for yourself."

"What's a very strange thing?" asked Erik.

"The elevator, sir."

The janitor was smiling a flat polite smile, as if he thought he represented a necessary intrusion.

"What elevator?" asked Inspector Erik, agitated.

"The service elevator," answered the cop, and he gestured again and grinned quickly, as if embarrassed. "There are strange sorts of shadows in it, sir." A brief pause. "Shadows!" he reiterated, paused again, and finished, "Burned into the elevator, sir." He nodded. "Into the wall of the elevator. Sort of like that wall at the Science Center. Where your shadow freezes."

NINETEEN

The white ceramic dog led Ryerson to Grenville Street, at the north edge of Yorkville, and then to a narrow alleyway between two sets of red-brick row houses. The dog paused and looked back. Ryerson had run a good distance and was out of breath, so he had to stop at the front of the alleyway.

When Ryerson had caught his breath, the ceramic dog loped to the middle of the long alleyway, stopped, and looked back again. Ryerson was closing quickly. The dog vanished in a microsecond's puff of flame, like flash paper.

Inspector Erik reached out and fingered the scorched area on the wall of the service elevator. He scowled, glanced at the uniformed cop standing just outside the elevator, then at the janitor, then once more at the scorched area, which he again touched. "I'll be damned," he said.

"It's what those two evil men did," proclaimed the janitor, nodding gravely.

"Then what?" asked Inspector Erik.

"Huh?" said the janitor.

"Then what did they do?"

"I don't know. I don't know what they did. I didn't see them do anything."

The scorched areas on the elevator wall were roughly manshaped. One was taller than the other, and they were connected at the arms, as if the two men had been standing very close to one another.

"Isn't it just like I said?" asked the uniformed cop. "Like the shadow wall at the Science Center?"

Inspector Erik looked at him oddly. "No. These are scorch marks, Officer. The wall at the Science Center doesn't actually *burn.*"

"Oh," the cop said, cowed. "You're right, of course. It isn't."

"I could smell 'em," offered the janitor, and cocked his head. "I still can."

Inspector Erik sniffed conspicuously. "Yes," he whispered.

The uniformed cop nodded. "Me, too." A brief pause. "It's the burned wall."

Early evening in downtown Toronto is a deluge of light and movement. It is not a terrifically loud time. Sounds are muffled, and even normally shrill voices seem quieter. This may very well be by comparison to the deluge of light and movement, magnified by so much glass and height and air. The three commingle to produce a sort of steady high-tech aura of power, the kind of power that whispers broadly and convincingly, *We are all very civilized here, and this is what we have built.*

Lenny Baker, very near the CN Tower in his nearly blind and awestruck search through the *presence,* was only dimly aware of this power and civility. He was also just dimly aware that he was hungry. He would do nothing about it, of course. He would follow wherever the *presence* led him.

Ryerson Biergarten, seated at a small table in a café in Old York, said to the waitress, "How long have I been here?"

She answered a little peevishly, "Two hours, close to three. More coffee?"

"Yes," he answered. "More."

She frowned and poured more coffee.

Ryerson nodded to himself. "You're right. "My dog is hungry."

The waitress paused in her pouring of the coffee. She shrugged—perhaps she had said something without realizing. She nodded at Creosote, seated next to Ryerson's right foot and looking hungrily at her. "Get him a burger?" she suggested, finished pouring the coffee, and looked questioningly at Ryerson.

"Yes." Ryerson glanced at her. "He'd like a burger." He reached down and scratched Creosote's chin.

"And you?" asked the waitress.

Ryerson glanced at her again, shook his head, and looked blankly at his coffee.

"Are you all right?" asked the waitress.

"No burger for me," Ryerson said, his head still turned. "Just one for my dog. Uncooked, of course."

"Yes, uncooked. Right away," said the waitress. "Are you sure you're all right?"

Ryerson shook his head but didn't look at her. "No. I'm not. There's something I've got to do, and I don't want to do it."

"A common complaint, eh?" said the waitress. "Uncooked hamburger for the pooch."

Ryerson looked at her. "Yes. For the pooch." He scooped Creosote up, stood, said, "In a minute or two," and moved off toward Yonge Street and the subway entrance there.

Down deep within himself, Fredrick Dunn wanted very badly to climb into his Jaguar and take it for a good fast spin on the back roads twenty miles north of Toronto. He needed that. He also wanted to swagger into some bar on Bloor Street and pick up a woman and take her home. And he wanted to write a letter to his sweet mother in Chicago, even if she wouldn't understand it; or, understanding it, wouldn't remember that he—Fredrick Dunn—was her son. Those were things that human beings did. Things that he had done when he was a human being.

It was sad to glance at his dark reflection in the shop windows. Sad to see the shape and movements that were human and know that it was a disguise that had been thrown over him, a disguise he had thrown over himself.

He would never again send anyone Christmas cards. That was something very human. People were always talking about what separated humans from animals. That did. Sending Christmas cards.

It was odd, but he felt spiritual. Cosmic. At one with the universe. The universe, after all, was as murderous as he—it swallowed stars, it ate galaxies, and he had absorbed some of that. It wasn't a need, it was reality—the only reality, too, because it lasted forever. And he had absorbed a piece of it. All humans could. Some others had, and they were well known to history.

So, too, would he absorb the creature walking with him, just as the creature had absorbed him, had moved his arms and legs about and made him do things in a way that he didn't want to do them. Like hide bodies in ceilings. For example, wrap bodies in plastic and hide them in ceilings and wait for them to fall on someone, *plop!*

That was a joke, wasn't it?

If so, then it was a cosmic joke because that creature was also spiritual, had absorbed some small digit of the universe, was cosmic, had once perhaps had bones and blood, as he—Fredrick Dunn—still did, or supposed he did. It was the costume of the universe itself—blood and bones, that small fragment of the universe wrapped up behind a face that grinned. Everyone grinned. And that was the key. He—Fredrick Dunn—had discovered what no one else anywhere had discovered, that he was a living, breathing fragment of the universe that swallowed galaxies whole.

He was a part of God.

So that creature walking with him was his servant.

Ryerson did not want to do this alone. It was a real struggle now even to keep his bearings—he had to say to himself, though not in so many words, *I am on a subway beneath Yonge Street in Toronto, and I am a part of the world that wakes up in the morning, and breathes and eats candy and elects people to public office.* Because he was beginning to feel strongly that he was a part of the other world that overlaid and encompassed and embraced all that, and embraced so much else.

I am beneath Yonge Street in Toronto, he told himself.

Above me now people are going to dinner. Some of those people are concerned with the color of their clothes, concerned that gray doesn't match with brown or blue with red. Some of them are wondering if the restaurant they're going to will accept credit cards, and some are worried that their cars are illegally parked and they'll get towed.

Also an old man in suspenders, a plaid shirt, and baggy gray pants misses his granddaughter whom he hasn't seen in some time. He believes that death will catch up with him before he sees her again.

It will. What can he do about it? A small hand will reach into him, seek out his heart and squeeze it to a stop. What can he do about it? The only hand he'll see will be his own, clutching desperately at his chest.

Small creatures at play in a world of human hearts.

But a woman is batting her eyelashes, too, or thinks she is, that that's what she's doing while she flirts. "Quaint," she thinks. "I am quaint in a world of the new."

Fredrick Dunn is in several different worlds at once, and has been for years.

So, too, is Lenny Baker, who sees the *presence* writhing about on the CN Tower against a backdrop of a thousand stars pulsing above and below, all around, embracing it.

The clumsy, the uninitiated, and the gauche are a part of all these worlds. The heroic are, too, and the mundane. How could it be otherwise?

Like Lenny Baker.

All of them dance in the air.

"Sir," the man said to Ryerson Biergarten, "your dog's resting his nose on me."

Ryerson said nothing.

The man said, "Do you hear me?" He was sitting beside Ryerson, on the window side of the subway car. He was a man of thirty-five, and he was dressed well for an evening of barhopping. He felt that he looked beautiful.

Ryerson stayed quiet.

The man lifted the sleeping Creosote's head gently and set it down so that Creosote's muzzle was on Ryerson's leg. Creosote's eyes fluttered open, closed; then he transferred his head back to the man's leg.

"Lord," the man whispered, and moved closer to the window so Creosote's head dropped into the space between Ryerson's leg and the man's leg. Creosote gurgled in his sleep, then hunkered forward so his snout was once again on the man's leg. "Dammit!" the man breathed. He was sure that Ryerson was sleeping, too, though his eyes were half-open. It was the way the man's wife slept, so it wasn't strange to him.

*　*　*

(Ryerson's soul was absent from the subway car. Fredrick Dunn's soul was absent from the street where he was walking. Their souls moved about high in the air above the CN Tower, each hidden from the other, as if they were in a vast dark maze where stars pulsed and the winds were fierce above them.)

The man in the seat next to Ryerson declared, "Your *dog* is an *annoyance,* sir!"

Ryerson looked uncomprehendingly at him.

"Oh, damn!" the man hissed. "He's drooled on me." The man swiped at his pants. Creosote woke with a start, gurgled, snorted, then curled up on Ryerson's lap.

Ryerson murmured, "I'm sorry."

The line had been broken. He was whole again.

"One dollar, sir."

Lenny Baker fumbled his wallet from the inside pocket of his white sports coat, pulled out a Canadian dollar, and handed it to the young woman behind the ticket counter at the base of the CN Tower. "I'm going all the way up," he mumbled.

"Sorry, sir?" She hadn't understood him.

He repeated himself. She understood him. "Yes, sir. To the Space Deck level. You'll be paying an additional dollar at the lower observation deck."

"Yes, I know."

"Enjoy yourself, sir."

He lumbered off to the elevator that would take him to the lower observation level, and pressed the UP button.

The elevator came moments later, and he got in, along with a young couple and an older man.

They started their ascent.

The elevator operator droned on about the statistics of the tower, about the duration of the ride on the exterior elevator, and one minute forty-five seconds later, the elevator stopped. It was at the lower observation level, 1,165 feet up. The doors opened. The young couple got out, then the older man. The elevator operator looked at Lenny and smiled. "Enjoy yourself, sir," he said.

Lenny said, "I don't want to be here."

"Would you like to go back down, sir?"

"No," Lenny said and got out.

TWENTY

On an enclosed walkway which spanned two sets of railroad tracks on the west side of the CN Tower, Fredrick Dunn stood arguing with the young man who had for so long possessed him.

Now that young man was whole. Complete.

His name was Steve Huckaby. A construction accident in Chicago six years earlier had brought death to him. That death had been the result of Chief Architect Fredrick Dunn's haste. It was a haste borne of greed.

Steve Huckaby had spent the last few moments of his life in an air dance, in the exhilaration of free-fall. Then his body had impacted with the earth.

And, at that moment, his soul had merged with the soul of Fredrick Dunn.

"Of course you're my servant," Fredrick Dunn insisted now, on the covered walkway over the railroad tracks on the west side of the tower.

"I ain't no one's *servant!*" Steve Huckaby insisted. He was blond, blue eyed, fair skinned, attractive. He wore faded blue jeans, a red plaid shirt and a pair of heavy steel-toed brown shoes. He was the perfect replica of his living self, and the few passersby moving briskly past on their way to Sparkles, the Sky-High Nightclub at the 1,165-foot level of the tower, were polite enough to ignore him and Fredrick Dunn and the argument going on.

"I'm a part of *God*!" shouted Fredrick Dunn.

"You ain't shit!" Huckaby sneered.

"I'm much more than shit!" countered Fredrick Dunn. "Much more than shit!"

Steve Huckaby grinned at him. "You got a shitty soul!"

"What the hell would you know about my soul?"

"I lived in it."

"You weren't invited."

"I didn't need to be."

They were close to the window that overlooked the moat which circled the tower. The heat radiating from them was beginning to turn the beige vinyl wall covering below the window a dull brown.

A passerby noticed the heat. She was a woman of sixty-eight, with keen senses, and she told herself that the heating system must be working overtime.

Heat existed around Steve Huckaby and Fredrick Dunn because a kind of forced and unnatural birth had occurred. Where only one entity had taken up space in the psychic atmosphere, now there were two. Friction was the result. The result of that friction was heat.

Fredrick Dunn shouted at Steve Huckaby, "*I* didn't want to wrap those people up in plastic and stick them in the ceilings!"

The old woman stopped when she heard that and looked back. Fredrick Dunn and Steve Huckaby were a dozen feet behind her. They were very involved in their argument and didn't notice her.

"What you do with *meat*," cried Steve Huckaby, "don't make no difference to the meat!"

"Well, by God," sputtered Fredrick Dunn, "that's damned . . . sick!"

"And you *loved* it!"

"It made me cringe! It made me squirm! I didn't *love* it!"

The old woman standing a dozen feet away kept up with the news, and the news about the "Toronto High Places Killer" was very familiar to her. She thought, listening to Steve Huckaby and Fredrick Dunn, *It's them!* and continued to listen, though with growing trepidation.

Steve Huckaby said, as a kind of loud, sly aside, "Listen, man, I was *in* you, I know what *you're* all about."

Fredrick Dunn was offended. "I'm a Christian!" he insisted.

"So the hell am I!" Steve Huckaby countered.

By now, the old woman was beginning to believe that she was overhearing two crazy people in some kind of spontaneous, free-associative argument. She was beginning to feel less and less that either of them was the actual "Toronto High Places Killer" when they both noticed her at the same time.

She smiled. She was a slight woman with a thin face and broad lips that were covered with dark red lipstick, so the smile, though small and nervous, looked very large and clownlike.

Steve Huckaby tilted his head at her. He sensed age in

her, and wisdom, and he respected it because she reminded him very much of his grandmother. He stared silently at her. She continued to smile back at him. She wanted desperately to reassure him, and Fredrick Dunn—who had also turned his head to stare at her—that she was very harmless, as harmless as a bunny, which was the phrase that came to her. But she couldn't speak. She knew, looking into Steve Huckaby's still blue eyes that he was something she had never dealt with before, not even in her nightmares, and she knew without actually thinking it that speaking to him would be like speaking to a steel wall. She also knew without thinking it that he had the moral sense of a wall.

"I *am* a Christian!" he insisted at her. He was becoming quite taken with the fact that she looked like his grandmother. He hadn't seen his grandmother in years.

"It makes no difference, though, about Christians," Fredrick Dunn said.

The woman's mouth dropped open, revealing sparkling white teeth and a pale pink tongue.

Two punk rockers strolled onto the walkway. One was a girl of fifteen who was wearing a tight black leather skirt and had bright orange hair; the other was a boy of seventeen who looked very much like her, except that he was wearing black leather pants and his orange hair had been cut into a Mohawk.

"Uh, something strange here, Brenda," he said.

Brenda nodded. "Sure," she said noncomittally.

"Awful hot, I'd say."

They hurried past and were over the hump of the walkway, on their way down the other side, approaching the area where the tickets to the tower were sold, when Fredrick Dunn and Steve Huckaby stopped their argument. It was a sense of urgency that stopped them. A sense of being crowded, of needing air. An awareness that the psychic atmosphere had become stifling. Fredrick Dunn equated it with the feeling a harried parent of many small children might get finding them flocking around his feet. Steve Huckaby merely felt breathless, though he hadn't taken a breath in years.

They walked quickly, men with a purpose, toward the area where tickets to the tower were sold. On their way, Steve Huckaby put his arm around the waist of the open-mouthed woman. "Hello, Grandmother," he said.

The heat around him was unbearable, and she could only gasp for air. He carried her along as if she were a rag doll. After a dozen yards, he let her go and she plopped to the beige indoor/outdoor carpet like a sack of laundry. The memory of his grandmother had sunk once again into the murky pool that held the memories of his life on earth. And he saw only the surface of that pool, dark and impenetrable. Now and again, memories floated like dead fish to the surface of the pool, and he peered wonderingly at them.

A woman with shoulder-length straight blond hair, a long, purposeful stride, and dressed in a voluminous, earth-colored skirt and a man's gray herringbone tweed jacket came onto the walkway and saw the old woman lying motionless, saw Fredrick Dunn and Steve Huckaby moving over the hump of the walkway, and she called to them, "Hey, there's a woman on the floor there!" They continued walking. "Dammit!" she called. "I said there's a woman lying there!" Still, they continued walking. The blond woman ran over to the old woman lying on the carpet, rolled her over, and looked at her face. She gasped and shrank back from what she saw. A scream built quickly in her throat. And tore loose.

"Woman screaming," said Derek Swade, the manager at a concession stand near the base of the tower, close to where tickets were sold and where Lenny Baker had bought his ticket ten minutes earlier. Swade was talking to a young woman named Marnie Heffer, his assistant manager.

Marnie said, "I heard it."

Derek shushed her. He heard another scream. "There's another one," he said.

"Yes," Marnie said. "What do you think it is, Derek?"

"I think it's a woman screaming."

"Do you think she's in trouble?"

"That's possible, yes."

"Do you think we should call security?"

The old woman had no face, nor any skull beneath the missing oval of her face. Nor any brain in the missing skull cavity. She had only darkness. No blood, no bone, no flesh. Only a simple, deep, and articulate oval of darkness where her face had been.

Words came out of that oval of darkness.

"Help me. Please help me!"

TWENTY-ONE

When he was on Front Street West, outside the entrance to the CN Tower, Ryerson Biergarten saw the *presence*. He remembered encountering it decades before and watching it in awe and wonder. He did not wonder now. He had a sense of it—of what it was—in the same way that he had a sense for the way electricity worked, and why comets sprouted tails.

He also sensed that there was great trouble within the CN Tower.

There were two sets of cement steps ahead. One, to his left, led to Waldo's Restaurant, the other led directly to the tower. Above the glass doors which led to the tower, white letters on the gray concrete read, CN TOWER, and below it, *LA TOUR CN,* and below that, ENTRANCE.

He went up the steps and through those doors. There was a short open area and another set of glass doors beyond.

He was carrying Creosote. He set the dog down, looked earnestly at him, and said, "Stay!" Creosote's flat, toothy face was alive with confusion. "Stay!" Ryerson repeated, settled on his haunches, and took Creo-

sote's face in his hands. He read not only confusion in the
dog, but a sense of abandonment, too. Ryerson shook his
head. "I'm sorry, pal. I'm going somewhere." He
stopped. Where *was* he going? Into the tower, yes, but
then where? He scratched Creosote's neck lovingly. The
dog inclined his head toward his master's hand—*I like
that. More!* Ryerson said again, "Stay!" then straightened and went quickly through the second set of glass
doors which would lead him to the tower. He looked
back.

Creosote hadn't budged.

Two uniformed cops cruising near L'Hotel, a few hundred feet away, got the first call: "Unspecified trouble at
the CN Tower. All available units respond at once."

"Charlie fourteen, Roger, am responding," one of the
uniformed cops called back, and within seconds the car
came to a halt in front of the same doors that Ryerson
had gone through moments before.

It was need that drove Steve Huckaby and Fredrick
Dunn now—the same sort of need that drives earth-
worms from the ground during a rain. The same need
that pushes a fetus from the womb.

The need for space and air.

But Steve Huckaby and Fredrick Dunn had other
needs, as well. The need for altitude. The need to return
to the place of their birth.

They stepped into the exterior elevator that would take
them 1,160 feet up to the Skypod observation level. The
operator gasped for breath and leaped from the elevator.

The doors closed.
The walls became hot.
The wiring sizzled.
The elevator stayed put.

At Sparkles, The Sky-High Nightclub, someone had suggested—after overhearing part of a phone conversation between the bartender and the tower's security people—that there was a fire at ground level. It was a suggestion that sent a number of people to the windows in an attempt to get a glimpse of the base of the tower. The attempt was in vain because the tower curved sharply inward below the windows. Still, people looked down, more than a few noting loudly that if there were indeed a fire, then fire trucks would be arriving.

A man spotted the police cruiser parked on Front Street West, in front of the tower's main entrance, its roof lights flashing. "There's a fire truck!" he called.

"No," said his date, "it's not a fire truck, it's a cop car."

"Where?" said a man at another window.

"There!" the woman said, nodding.

"Where?" he asked again.

"Is it a fire truck?" someone else shouted.

"There's a fire truck down there!" someone yelled.

"No, it's a cop car."

Another cruiser appeared.

"Two fire trucks!" someone called.

The bartender bellowed, "There is no fire!"

But he'd said the magic word, of course. *Fire.* Then he repeated it. "There is no fire. Please don't panic!" He had

a good low voice, a voice full of confidence and authority, but he'd put great stress on the words "fire" and
"panic," and it was that stress which pushed people farther toward the windows in a vain search for flames at
the base of the tower.

"Get *away* from the goddamned windows!" the bartender bellowed.

"I can't see a friggin' thing!" someone yelled.

"What if there really is a fire?" someone else shouted.

"Christ, then we'd be trapped."

"There is *no damned fire!*" the bartender insisted. He
came around quickly from behind the bar and stood
behind the line of people—there were several dozen of
them at the windows—and said again, "There is no fire!"

"But there are fire trucks!"

"Will you for God's sake listen to me!" the bartender
bellowed.

A few people turned to listen. The rest kept their eyes
on the two police cars on Front Street West. The bartender shouted, to be heard above the hubbub of grim
speculation in the large room, "Even if there was a fire,
which there isn't, there's no way it could reach up here.
Think about it! There's eleven hundred and sixty feet of
cement between any fire—and there isn't a fire—and us.
Eleven hundred and sixty feet of cement, for Christ's
sake!"

The room quieted. His argument was rational and
convincing.

The bartender smiled, pleased that he could be so per-
suasive. Then a man asked him, "But if there is a fire,
does that mean we have to *walk* down?"

The bartender wasn't sure at first how to answer the question. There were two elevators, exterior and interior. Another elevator led to the Space Deck, 400 feet above, but it didn't go down from where they were. He said, "Sure, in a fire you walk down!"

"My God!" someone said. "The bartender said there's a fire, and we've got to walk down!"

"Holy shit!" someone yelled. "We're trapped up here!"

"There's no damned fire!" yelled the bartender.

Lenny Baker was standing motionless in a corridor outside Sparkles. He was motionless because he was incredibly frightened, and he was frightened because he felt as if he were in two different worlds at the same time and he was familiar with only one of them—the world where people nearby were working themselves into a panic, the world where "communication wands" rested on the windows that overlooked Toronto (and if a person held one of the wands to his ear and stood close to the window, he could get a speech about some aspect of the tower: its construction, history, et cetera), the world where his bladder had been threatening to let go for an hour. But he was not familiar with that other world, the world where the *presence* existed, the world that was as new and strange and enticing to him as color would be to a blind man.

So he stood motionless, afraid to move, uncertain of where he might go if he did move.

He was whimpering, too, out of fear. He did not hear the doors to the stairs being pushed open. They were down a short hall, around a corner, and the tower was so well constructed that sound did not travel well in it. But though he did not hear the door open, he sensed that something murderous and strange had just entered his world of panic, his world of swollen bladders and communication wands. His world 1,160 feet above the earth.

"What am I doing here?" he whispered.

He turned his head stiffly to the right.

Steve Huckaby and Fredrick Dunn appeared around the corner, from down the short hallway which led to the stairs.

They were wrapped in the *presence,* the fog, as if wrapped in cocoons.

Lenny stayed very still as they approached.

The old woman was still pleading, "Help me, please help me!" when Ryerson Biergarten happened upon her. And when he bent over and peered into the dark, impenetrable oval that had been her face, he tried to reassure her. "You are still with us," he whispered. But he knew that it was a lie. She was, perhaps irrevocably, where he soon would be—the same world that Lenny Baker had one foot in, the world that had produced Steve Huckaby and Fredrick Dunn. The world that now was taking them back.

Ryerson straightened.

From behind him, he heard, "Hold it right there!"

Dammit! he thought, and turned and looked. A cop was at the top of the hump of the walkway, twenty feet from him, under a lighted, overhanging sign—one of twenty in the walkway, each bearing a different message—which advertised the musical *The Little Shop of Horrors.*

Ryerson nodded at the woman at his feet and shook his head. "You can't help her—don't try to help her," he said.

"Hands where I can see them!" the cop ordered.

"My advice," Ryerson said, "would be to leave this woman right where she is. Don't touch her."

"I said put your hands where I can see them!" the cop repeated, and raised his pistol slightly. This is what he could see: Ryerson Biergarten, hands at his sides, left hand hidden by his pant leg and the bottom of his brown sport jacket. The woman lying on her back, feet together, arms out from her body a little. Her head was turned toward him, but Ryerson's foot hid most of it.

The cop, gun still pointed stiffly at Ryerson, took a few quick, nervous steps forward. The woman's face became visible to him. He did not believe what he was seeing. He said to Ryerson, "Good Lord, what's she got on her face?"

"Nothing," Ryerson answered.

The cop took several more quick, nervous steps forward. "She's got something all over her face! What in the hell *is* that?"

"There's nothing on her face," Ryerson said. "Don't touch her."

The cop leveled his gun even more stiffly at Ryerson. "Is that some kind of threat?"

"It's not a threat."

Several more people appeared in the hallway. One was the cop's partner, who had gone up the left-hand stair-

way at the entrance to the tower—it led to Waldo's Restaurant. That cop took up a position near his partner,
drew his gun, and pointed it at Ryerson. He did not
immediately focus on the face of the woman lying at
Ryerson's feet. From his vantage point, her face was
partially hidden. He was new to the Toronto Police Department, and what consumed him now was the fact that
this was the first time he'd drawn his weapon.

"What do we have here, Stan?" he said out of the
corner of his mouth.

Stan's gaze was transfixed by the woman's face. He
could only shake his head in response and mutter an
incoherency.

The next to appear behind Ryerson as he faced the two
cops was the CN Tower's head of security, a beefy man
named Allen who was wearing a white shirt, black pants,
and spit-shined black shoes. He carried no weapons, but
liked very much to act as if he did. "Okay," he barked,
"what the hell's going on here?" He had been summoned
by the blond woman in the voluminous earth-colored
skirt who had screamingly sought out the first official-
looking person she could find.

Another security guard appeared and stopped just behind Allen. He focused at once on the face of the woman
at Ryerson's feet, and whispered, "God, what's she got
on her face there?"

Ryerson realized he had nowhere to go. He had supposed he would be going up into the tower, after Fredrick Dunn. But he knew that that was not about to
happen now.

The cop ordered again, "Hands where I can *see* them!"

"What the hell is going on here?" Allen barked.

"What the hell's she got all over her face?" asked the security guard.

And Ryerson reached down, toward the woman, and put the tips of his fingers into the darkness where her face should have been, from where he could still hear the words "Help me, please help me!"

He had no concrete idea what would happen to him.

He felt a sudden queasiness in the pit of his stomach. He felt a sudden, screeching pain sear his arm.

Then he collapsed face-forward over the body of the woman.

TWENTY-TWO

The fear that swept over Allen when he rolled Ryerson off the woman and looked into the darkness where Ryerson's face should have been was like a physical blow. He stumbled backward, arms wide, hands in a mad search for something to steady himself. "Call someone!" he whispered. His hand found a window ledge. He grabbed it. "For God's sake, call someone." He looked at the two cops; both still had their weapons drawn. "Call someone," he blubbered at them. "Please call someone!"

At Sparkles, the Sky-High Nightclub, an expectant calm had settled over the people who had been huddled at the windows. While the bartender made a phone call to security, a few of those people wandered back to their seats. One of them, a young man, was the first to catch a glimpse of Steve Huckaby and Fredrick Dunn. He screamed a long, ragged scream—the kind a man makes in anticipation of great and imminent pain.

Others in the bar turned and looked. They saw Steve Huckaby and Fredrick Dunn, too, and some of them screamed the way the man was screaming, and some of them sat very still, and some of them smiled, thinking— hoping—that what they were seeing was only a show of some kind, some new attraction at the Sky High Night-club, and some fainted. One, a beautifully dressed man of thirty, slammed the side of his head into the edge of a table and was dead within moments. Two brothers vaca-tioning from New Jersey at the nightclub "in search of honeys" pulled handguns out of shoulder holsters and trained them on Steve Huckaby and Fredrick Dunn. "Holy Jesus," said one of the men. "Look at those poor slobs on fire!"

"Yeah," said his brother, "they gotta be sufferin' awful!"

And they both fired.

One of the bullets struck a woman in the back of her head, ricocheted from her skull, and passed cleanly through a window. Several seconds later, the bullet landed on the hood of a Jeep CJ4 passing 1,160 feet below, on Front Street West. The other bullet embedded itself in a wall after passing through Fredrick Dunn.

He was not aware of the bullet. He was not aware of the heat. He was aware only of his need for space and air. Aware of too much light around him. Aware that there were faces swimming before him, and faces swimming in his memory, too, although he did not recognize them.

He was also aware of pain, as if he were being squeezed on all sides at once. The same sort of pain a newborn might feel moments before it emerges from the womb.

Steve Huckaby was feeling the same kind of pain.

The same need for space and air.

And both of them realized at once that their need was not going to be satisfied here, in this place.

They had to go up. Farther up into the tower.

Ryerson Biergarten felt something solid beneath his feet. He felt cold air moving around him, and he heard the distant muttering of many voices. But he could see very little, as if he had just come in from bright sunlight. He tried to speak. "What is . . ." he said, but he knew that no one would hear him, because his voice was hollow and weak, as if he were speaking into a pillow.

His eyes began to adjust to the darkness. Shapes appeared around him. They were dull red against black, the shapes of people clustered nearby, and they were shouldering closer to him.

"What is—" he said again, intending to ask, *What is this place?* but he was stopped by a sudden shrieking wail that arose from the people drawing close.

He realized that he was crouching, as if he were hiding in a closet under a low shelf. He straightened slowly. His eyes adjusted further to the darkness and the people who were clustered around him became a more vibrant red, the darkness beyond them a richer, deeper darkness, as if it were the darkness of space itself. But it was not that kind of darkness. It was a living, violent darkness, like the darkness inside a storm, a darkness so deep that the cold air moving around him could have been its breath.

"What . . ." he began, and again a shriek rose up from the people shouldering closer to him.

"What is this place?" he said, but again the people shrieked as soon as he spoke. "Who *are* you?" he wailed.

And they shrieked over his words, as if wounded by them.

The bartender at Sparkles was all but incoherent. He could barely hold the telephone. "What do you mean we can't use the stairs?" he said.

"They're hot," answered an officious male voice on the other end. "The east stairs seem to be okay, but our suggestion would be to stay put until we're sure. Do you understand?"

"Hot?" said the bartender. "What do you mean 'hot'? Get us the fuck down from here!"

"We have people on their way up to you now. It's going to take a while. We've got to cool the stairs. We've got to go up a hundred and twelve stories."

"And the elevators are out?" the bartender asked incredulously.

"Yes. I'm sorry. They are. They're out." A pause. "Do you have a doctor up there?"

"A doctor? What the hell for? We have dead people up here."

"So there is no doctor?"

"Yes, there are doctors. They say that there are people dead up here. Get us down, please get us down!"

"We're doing what we can . . ."

"And meanwhile people are dying—"

"We have help on the way up to you."

Lenny Baker wasn't sure whether he was moving or standing still. He thought he was trying to feel his way in the darkness, but he had no way of being sure of that because he felt buoyant, as if he were afloat and unmoving—like a fly caught in a web—and the connection between his brain and body had become spongy, as if the temperature of his skin were exactly the temperature of the air.

He had no sensation of breathing, of the need to inhale and exhale.

He could see movement in the darkness, as if the darkness itself were in motion. He could hear the distant muttering of many voices, like a flight of geese high overhead.

He could hear Ryerson's voice distantly, too. "Who are you?" it said.

"Rye?" Lenny called. "Are you there?"

"Who are you?" Ryerson said again.

Steve Huckaby and Fredrick Dunn moved like ghosts through the closed doors of the elevator. Then they moved up, through the ceiling of the elevator, through the shaft of the tower above the elevator, and farther, past the corridor where a thousand small copper plaques bore the names of members of the Sky-High Club, past people caught on the Space Deck—on the other side of the blood-red elevator doors, waiting to go down—"Is there a phone?" one asked. "I think there must be something wrong—where's a damn phone?"—past the graffiti-littered poster of the Matterhorn (THIS ELEVATOR IS GOOD TO THE LAST DROP), behind it, beyond it, up through the shaft and into the density of the concrete, into the point of the tower.

And up. Still up. Like ghosts, into the darkness and cold and wind above the tower.

To their place of safety.

The place of their birth.

Light exploded into Ryerson's eyes, and he screamed because it was painful.

Then, as quickly, the light was gone.

And darkness returned.

But the sudden flash of light had shown him . . . architecture. *Was that right?*

No, he realized. He hadn't seen *architecture,* he had seen a landscape, a backdrop to the people shouldering closer to him. A landscape revealed in the sudden blinding and painful flash of light.

"Ryerson?" he heard. "Where are you?" It was Lenny Baker's voice. Ryerson thought, *Where am I? I haven't a clue!*

He felt suddenly as if he were in a chair and he was slipping out of it.

While, about him, the people shouldered closer.

They would never reach him, he knew, though he didn't know how he knew it. He hadn't a clue about that, either.

But yes, he realized at once, he did. He'd had clues all his life. It's what he was himself—a clue to this place and to these people shouldering closer to him. He realized that if he were a religious man, he would believe that this was hell. Or heaven. But what did he know? What could any of the living know about this place? It was like expecting an infant to know what it was to be old, to know the purpose and meaning and mechanics of its own birth and its own death.

Entities were born here.

Entities like Fredrick Dunn and Steve Huckaby.

And perhaps he, Ryerson Biergarten, had been born here, too.

Inspector Erik barked at Allen, the chief of security at the CN Tower, "How many are up there?"

Allen looked very confused. "I'm sorry, Inspector"—he smiled a quivering, apologetic smile—"we're not sure. It's not something we keep close track of. But the stairs are being hosed down. The heat should dissipate—"

Inspector Erik caught the attention of a firefighter running past. "How soon before we can get up those stairs?"

The firefighter slowed a little, shook his head once—Inspector Erik wasn't sure what the gesture meant—and continued running.

"Damn!" the inspector whispered, watched the firefighter a few moments, then turned to Allen and said, "Men's room?"

"There are several," Allen answered.

"The nearest one."

Allen nodded in the direction the firefighter had run. "Past the concession area, to the left."

"But are they *alive*?" asked a reporter for the *Toronto Star,* referring to Ryerson Biergarten and the woman he had fallen on.

Dr. John Lloyd nodded. "They're breathing. That's all I can tell you." Ryerson's body was not visible from the area where the bank of reporters stood, twenty feet inside the Front Street West entrance to the tower, near

Waldo's Restaurant. "We don't want to move them—we don't know if that would be wise. For the moment, we're leaving them where they are."

"And the people in the tower?" shouted a reporter.

Dr. Lloyd shook his head. "I know nothing of that situation. That is an ongoing situation, a developing situation, and it is outside my purview . . ."

"Sorry?" shouted another reporter.

"I have no idea what's happening to the people in the tower," Dr. Lloyd clarified.

"I see something up there," said a man standing near a window at Sparkles.

"What do you see?" asked his date.

"Movement," he said.

She put her face into the window, looked up. "I don't see anything, Charlie. I see darkness."

"No," he said. "There's more than that. It's like heat . . . waves of heat."

"I see it," she announced. "Like the air's moving."

"Waves of heat," Charlie said again. "See, the stars are twinkling from it."

"That's what stars *do,* Charlie."

"More! They're twinkling more. Look, can't you see that?"

"But what could be up there?"

"Nothing at all," Charlie answered.

Ryerson thought he was at a great altitude. He could see nothing to suggest that that was true, but it was what he felt.

"Ryerson?" he heard. "Are you there?" Lenny Baker's voice, but Ryerson was hearing it as if over a telephone line, over a great distance.

And the people shouldered closer, ever closer, but never so close that they could touch him—as if they were merely a huge panoramic picture and his perspective on it changed constantly; the picture got bigger or he got smaller.

And as close as they were, their eyes were always lost in shadow. He wondered whether they had eyes at all.

"Ryerson?" Lenny Baker pleaded, and Ryerson heard anguish in the man's voice.

Then there was another explosion of light, the same as before, and it hurt him.

In it he saw the same landscape, the same backdrop—horizon, earth, sky. But little else.

Another pulse of light stabbed at him. He swiped at it as if it were an insect. And the people shouldering closer moved off.

Another pulse of light. Another. Another. They piled up in geometric progression, like the revolutions of an engine starting, and with each pulse, Ryerson's pain weakened, until, at last, he was in a very rapidly pulsing daylight.

Alone.

Except for two men standing together on the vast empty plain between him and the horizon. Two men he thought he could reach out and touch, as if they were merely distant figures in a painting.

They stood very still.

Ryerson reached for them, saw his arm go up at right

angles to his body, saw his fingers stretch, thought, *I am looking at someone else's arm, someone else's fingers!* But he knew that he was looking at his own arm, at his own fingers. But they were reaching into an alien world, a world he had trespassed in, but was not a part of—a world that he had never been a part of, a world that could produce creatures like Fredrick Dunn and Steve Huckaby and then set them loose—by accident or by design—on his own world.

And now they had come back to their own world.

To wait.

His world—Ryerson's world—had spit them out, had pushed them back.

So now they waited.

Waited to do what they had been created to do, to perform, to function, to *be*—just as the black widow spider waits for weeks under a porch for the hapless fly or the errant hand.

So these two entities waited.

Perhaps they were not even aware of time, or change. Did they have memories here? Ryerson wondered. Were they a part of someone's photo albums, boys dressed in white for their first communions, boys sniggering at cameras, boys growing into men, men growing into . . . this?

To wait.

To be—again—what this strange world had designed them to be.

But he knew that he was only guessing.

And he knew, as well, that if he waited here and watched, that this awful world, this place where evil was created, would take him for itself.

"Ryerson!" Lenny called. "Come back to us!"

He called back, "My God, I want to!"

He had gotten himself into something far beyond his comprehension, Lenny realized. It made him feel afraid, alone, vulnerable. It made him feel as if he were blind and in a room cluttered with bottles of nitroglycerine. How could he move? Where would he go? He was stuck. The only thing he could do was reach out and touch whatever was near.

He did it.

Ryerson reflexively grabbed the hand offered him and yanked hard on it.

It was like yanking at a wall.

Dr. Lloyd, bending over Ryerson's body, whispered, "His face!"

Tom, the medical technician standing by, said, "Sorry, doctor."

"It's coming back," Lloyd declared.

Tom leaned over for a better look. He saw a ghostly image in the darkness where Ryerson's face should have been, and he straightened and retreated, in awe, to the opposite side of the walkway.

The hand Ryerson clutched was cold and hard, like the hand of a dead man. But it was *himself,* he realized, who was the dead man, *himself* who was trying to reach back into the world of the living.

There was a ring on the hand; he recognized it. It was

Lenny Baker's ring, and Lenny's hand. He held very tightly to it.

Lenny thought that the hand he clutched in the darkness was barely there, as if he were clutching a leaf. "Ryerson!" he called. "Hold on!"

The light vanished as abruptly as if a switch had been thrown.

And with the darkness came again the distant muttering of many voices.

"Lenny!" Ryerson called. "For God's sake . . ."

He felt pressure at his arms, his rib cage, the sides of his legs, his temples, as if he were being forced into a tube.

He was feeling the pressure of hands and legs and bodies against him.

He was being pushed out. Expelled.

Just as *his* world had expelled Steve Huckaby and Fredrick Dunn, so *this* world and its people were expelling him.

The pressure increased.

And he felt not so much that he was being pushed *out* as *in.* Into himself. Into his own soul.

And still he felt Lenny Baker's cold hand, and he clung hard to it. "Help me!" he screamed. "For God's sake, help me!"

"Dammit!" Lenny screamed. "Dammit, Rye!"

Ryerson heard a low, grisly crunching sound. The

sound of his own soul yielding to the pressure of the creatures that ruled here.

Then the face of Fredrick Dunn was before him, *within* him in the darkness. And the anguish on it was like a layer of sweat. Words came from it; "Tell my mother I love her."

Lenny felt Ryerson's hand melt away, as if it were water. "God, no!" he screamed.

On the walkway over the railroad tracks, Ryerson Biergarten groped blindly at the air and struggled to his feet, pushed Dr. Lloyd away, stumbled to a window, and screamed.

He had returned.

TWENTY-THREE

Thank you, Lenny," Ryerson said, and shook his hand.

"For what?" Lenny asked, because he had no concrete idea of exactly what had happened in the CN Tower. In his memory, it was like the bottom layer of graffiti on a wall that has fifty years of graffiti layered on it.

"For being . . . persistent!" Ryerson explained, and got into his Volkswagen. It was parked in a public parking lot on Front Street West, not far from the tower. Creosote—retrieved two days earlier from the Toronto City Pound—lay sleeping in the backseat. Ryerson closed the door, rolled the window down and looked at Lenny. "For being human," he added.

"Sure I'm human," Lenny said, smiling. "Aren't we all?"

Ryerson grinned and said, "See you."

"Are you coming back?" Lenny asked.

"Yes. I'll be back. This is a beautiful city."

Lenny grinned. "We like it." His grin faded. He lifted

his pudgy chin to indicate the CN Tower. "What's up there, Rye?"

Ryerson shook his head. "Nothing's up there, Lenny." He shrugged. "Nothing unique, anyway."

"I don't understand."

"It's like . . . a blanket, I think. It covers all of us."

Lenny stooped over and put his hands on the bottom of the driver's window. "I still don't understand, Rye. And I don't think you do, either."

Ryerson smiled.

"Well," Lenny coaxed, "do you?"

"If I said that I didn't, I'd be lying. And if I said that I did, I'd be lying, too." He shook his head in confusion. "I'm a part of it; we're *all* a part of it." A pause. "We exist in it. We do what we have to do. We try to understand ourselves." He shook his head again. "Do you remember a speech I made once, Lenny?" He glanced at the sleeping Creosote. "About him, and the wolf inside him. About possession."

"I remember."

Ryerson grinned. "It may or may not have been bullshit. If it was, then it wasn't intended. I try to say the things that I think are true."

"Don't we all?"

"Yes." He paused, then; "Dammit!"

"Sorry?" Lenny said, surprised.

"We're thrust here from *some*where, Lenny."

"I don't understand that."

"Well *I* do!"

Lenny straightened. He looked silently at Ryerson for

a moment, glanced at the tower, then at Mario's Restaurant, a half-block south. "I'm going to get some lunch," he said.

Ryerson ignored him. "We're thrust here from *some-*where, Lenny. We do what we have to do, and then we go back to wherever we came from. It's simple."

"If you say so, Rye."

Ryerson looked at him for a couple of seconds, then he said, "No, Lenny. I *want* it to be simple. I *want* it to be easily pinned down. I want to say that there is *this* place"—he pointed at the ground—"and that there is *that* place"—he lifted his chin, as Lenny had, to indicate the area above the tower—"and we are all shuffled back and forth somehow between those places. It would be . . . orderly."

"The universe isn't orderly," Lenny told him.

"The universe is perfect," Ryerson said. "It works, so it's perfect. And there is nothing—anywhere—that says we have to understand it."

"But you do?" Lenny asked.

Ryerson started the Volkswagen. "Enjoy your lunch," he shouted over the clatter of the little engine, and realized that "Enjoy your lunch" was one of the first things he had ever said to Lenny.

"Sorry?" Lenny said because he hadn't heard him.

Ryerson shouted, "Enjoy your lunch," and put the Volkswagen in gear. "Thank you for being there."

Lenny continued to look confused.

Ryerson pulled away, stopped at Front Street West, turned right, drove past the tower.

Creosote woke, scrambled to the front of the car, and settled down on Ryerson's lap. Ryerson scratched idly at the dog's ears. Creosote gurgled.

"Hi, pal," Ryerson said.